From the Void

From the Void

Energematrice6
THE EPIMYTH INTERVAL I

JARED N. MICHAUD

From the Void

Energematrice6 — The Epimyth Interval I

ISBN: 978-1-965598-00-9 ebook
ISBN: 978-1-965598-01-6 paperback
ISBN: 978-1-965598-02-3 hardback

Cover Design
Sarah Michaud Illustration and Design
sarahlynnmichaud.wixsite.com/my-site

Interior Design
Jared N. Michaud
jarednmichaud.com

Other Works
by Jared N. Michaud

Energematrice6

Brightstar

From the Void

The Vale of Mysteries

Mythologia

Winternight

Il Alka E'Talania

Free Ebooks!
(And Value4Value)

The entire Energematrice6 library is available for free in ebook form at https://www.e6universe.com.

I offer this to you primarily because as a young person I wasn't able to afford to buy books, and was limited to what I could find at the library or, as I grew into my teens, online.

Please take advantage of it! Read everything!

If you enjoy my writing, I would appreciate it if you can return some value to me by buying something (like a physical book) to say "thank you" when you're able.

I hope you enjoy the Energematrice6 Universe!

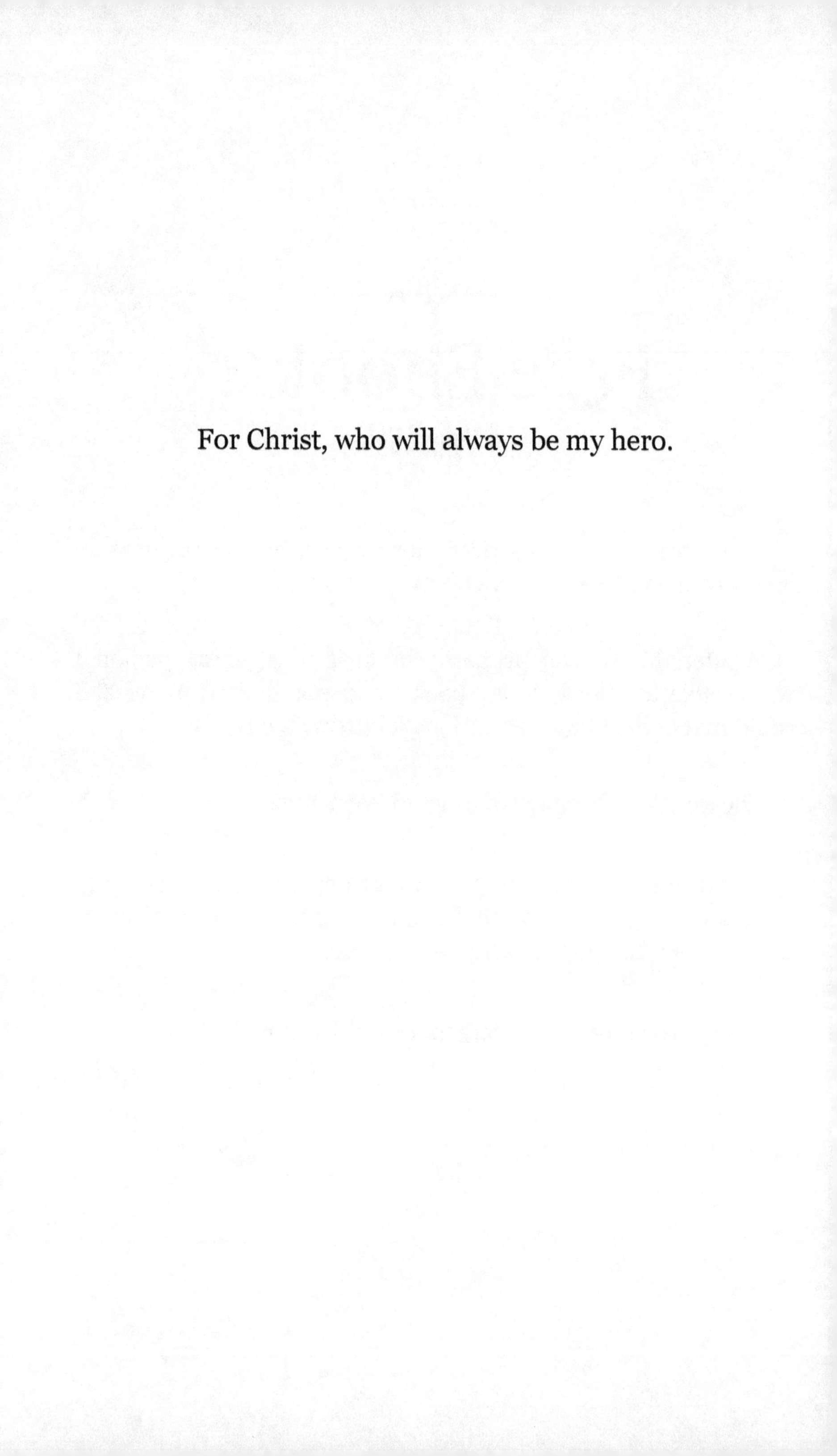

For Christ, who will always be my hero.

Acknowledgments

I sincerely hope that every time I publish a new book I'll have more people to thank than I did the last time. As I recently told a friend, when someone is willing to help me with these stories—to enjoy and even love them—I come to value their contributions to the work even more than my own. With so many people who have played a small part at some stage, especially in one of these short stories, I'm sure to forget people. If that's you, my apologies. Thank you to everyone who contributed.

To Mary—As always, you contributed more than your share, from feeding me and taking care of me when I'm too focused to think of anything else, to being my reader of first resort and primary sounding board. Thank you.

To my beta-reader-in-chief, Nick—I don't know what I'd do without your perspective. Your genuine love of the stories I write is more of an encouragement to me than you know. Thank you.

To my lore collector, Multaan—Your attention to detail and critical eye has made your input indispensible. You are a blessing to me. Thank you.

To Greg—Thank you for sticking with me and doing everything you can, even when you're dealing with far too much yourself. As always, you are as much a brother as a friend. Thank you.

To Luke, Aaron, Ben, Natalie, and Tim McKay—Thank you for being my editors and beta readers. Even when I can think of specific places where you improved the final product, the confidence I get from having you check my work is of yet more value. Thank you.

To Sarah—Every new person who reads my work is thanks to your work at least as much as mine. You are an artist as well as a designer. Thank you.

To all of the folks who participated in the kickstarter (I'm not including your names because I don't want to dox you), thank you. Not much happens in this world without financial support. Hopefully this is worth your wait.

There are so many others who have provided everything from moral support to key ideas, and I appreciate you all. Thank you, to everyone who has been a part of the Energematrice6 universe thus far. Here's to many more years and many more stories.

Finally and always, to the Father of the heavenly lights in whom the whole world consists and finds its value. No thanks can be enough.

Thousands of years before the arrival of the Brightstar, escapees from dying Earth were transported through the darkness beyond reality itself to a new home. Though the colonists' physical safety was never in danger following their arrival in the Aurora Galaxy, the little group struggled to confront the horrors of a dark past that some wished simply to forget.

Meanwhile, one-time governor Paul Casisia and his twin children, Jon and Rachel, looked to defend this last free colony of humanity from a future far darker than they could imagine.

Genesis of a Dark Age

Year 4 NST – Aterria, Aurora Galaxy

You can't keep taking those kids out into the void, Paul. They should be spending time with children their own age!" Matilda Mathison's voice seemed too high-pitched to be real, even coming from her slight frame. Today, her expression was particularly grim, as if it lay upon her shoulders alone to right the wrongs in the universe.

She took her presumed role very seriously.

"No one else has the strength to watch the Redoubt or ensure we aren't attacked unaware, Matilda. Who should I leave them with when I'm gone?"

"They should have a mother, and you know it!" Paul Casisia didn't flinch. The hurt in his eyes was too old and well-worn for that, but his expression dulled for a moment under her onslaught.

"Shrewtongue." Rachel Casisia whispered sidelong to her twin brother, Jon. He snorted in amusement, but Paul shot Rachel a sharp, remonstrative look. He shouldn't have heard her at all, from where she and Jon sat yards away on the picnic blanket. Maybe he was using Energematrice6. With her dad, she still couldn't quite tell.

Either way, the glance only lasted a spare moment before he focused his attention on Mrs. Mathison fully and asked, wryly, "Who should they be spending time with, Matilda? The other kids all know exactly who they are and how old they are. Everybody who came through the Dark with us is still aging and we're not. I notice you've got a few more gray hairs than you did that day." Paul shook his head ruefully to take any sting out of his comment. "I'm not arguing with you, Matilda, but the universe we live in is far from perfect."

She barked a single laugh, her tone half humorous and half grim, "Which one? We've been reborn, Paul. The old world is gone. We've left evil men like Lastis Ralond behind us! It's time to shed the remnants of that old world; none of that darkness can reach us here."

Paul shook his head, now entirely grim. "I wish I could agree, Matilda. We escaped from Earth, but human nature is the same here as anywhere else. Besides..." He trailed off, obviously deep in thought.

Matilda waited for him to finish, then when he didn't she huffed gently and shook her head, half smiling. "Well, don't be gone too long, Paul Casisia. There are still some of us who remember..." She paused for a long moment, her attention an unfathomable distance—and many years— away, then shook her head again. She seemed on the verge of speaking, but something distracted her and she craned her neck, looking down the slope toward the edge of the park.

A moment later, Jon and Rachel heard what had distracted Mrs. Mathison and craned their own necks, trying to see past the trees that marked the boundary of the park. It was the sound of a crowd, and it was rapidly drawing near.

Paul sighed, then glanced over his shoulder toward Jon and Rachel with a sour expression.

Jon grumbled, "More company."

The first members of the crowd began to filter through the trees toward them, and Paul's sigh became a concerned frown. Their eyes were hard, and Rachel saw a lot of unhappy faces among those walking toward them through the brilliantly-green grass.

Paul grumbled, "Can't we just have a picnic?"

Matilda laughed, then pointed toward Hope One, a hundred yards behind them, stretching toward the sky like a gigantic, silver finger.

Rachel grinned. "Daddy, you set Hope down in the middle of the city *park!* What did you expect?"

Paul grimaced. "It isn't like we've never done it before."

Rachel rolled her eyes again. "Five years ago. And they pitched a fit then, too."

Paul grinned at her as he rose to his feet once more. "Being a 'celebrity' has to have some perks, doesn't it?" His dutiful turn to meet those coming toward them hid his teasing smirk.

The rest of the crowd began to break through the trees and Matilda cleared her throat uncomfortably. "I think I'd better go. Good luck, Paul. Mind what I said about these young ones."

Mrs. Mathison immediately started off down the hill the other direction, away from the crowd.

Rachel frowned as she eyed first the oncoming mass of people then Mrs. Mathison's retreating back. "That was abrupt. I wonder why she's so anxious?"

Then, the first shouts reached them. Most of the words were lost to distance, but "tech" and "ship" came from more than one throat. Rachel even thought she recognized a face or two, but any familiarity was overcome by a creeping sense of alarm. Why were these people here?

Her dad obviously wondered the same thing. She saw him starting toward the nearest of them with an annoyed expression. She couldn't make out their words, but when the man gestured toward Hope One, it was clear that he wasn't happy.

She scanned, looking for anyone her own age she might recognize—or, she amended to herself, a few years older than she was. Last time she saw any of these people, they would have been two years younger. She might actually be able to learn more than her dad could, if she could find the right teen.

There was no one she recognized, but she spotted something that gave her pause. Most of the crowd was staring at Hope behind her, or moving purposefully toward Paul, some with angry looks on their faces. One little girl, though, even younger than Rachel's apparent thirteen years, was darting from one cluster of people to the next.

Her movements were furtive, as if she were hiding. Looking around, though, Rachel couldn't see anyone who was obviously chasing her. Rachel had wished for a younger sister—or even a younger brother—for as long as she could remember. Her mom had died when she was very small, though, and unless her dad decided to adopt, the prospects of that were slim.

She was a pushover and she knew it—and she should probably mind her own business besides. Still, something about the obviously-frightened girl, darting from one cluster of people to another, called to her.

Rachel sighed and rose to her feet, then spoke over her shoulder to Jon, "I'll be back. Don't let them raid our picnic."

Rachel eyed the people around them, most of whom had stopped some way back from Hope and were staring up at the vessel, seeming almost frightened. None of them were looking at her and Jon—one of the perks of being 'just kids.' Nobody would notice her until she said something they thought was out of character.

Rachel moved among the knots of people, looking for the girl. A moment later Rachel found her again. She actually bumped into the shorter girl as the child—she couldn't have been more than six—rounded a little group of staring onlookers, her head turned to look back. The girl started violently, then stared up into Rachel's face with wide eyes. Rachel grabbed her wrist and put a finger over her lips.

For a moment, the girl looked as if she might wrench her arm free and bolt, but Rachel motioned toward the blanket where Jon was sitting, and after considering for a moment, the girl nodded hesitantly. Rachel quickly led her back to the picnic site and sat, pulling the other girl down next to her.

When Rachel released her wrist, she again looked like she might bolt, but Rachel raised an eyebrow and asked, "What are you afraid of?"

The girl sucked in a breath, then hugged her knees to her chest, looking like she might cry. "They're coming."

"Who's coming?" Jon was looking around now, eyes sharp as he scanned the crowd. "Where are your parents?"

"Gone. Not my parents. Seebur…"

The girl's breathing was fast and shallow and Rachel sighed in exasperation. Then, after a moment, she said, "OK. Slow down. What's your name? Who's chasing you?" She put an arm around the younger girl, hoping to ease her obvious fright, and after a moment the girl seemed to relax at least a little, leaning in to Rachel.

"Annie…I don't know what they are, but… They're after Seebur. Have you seen him?" She looked up at Rachel pleadingly.

Rachel, meanwhile, had been looking for her dad. She finally spotted him, down the slope, talking with one of the crowd.

"What are you afraid of, Annie?"

Annie looked around again, obviously frightened, but didn't answer immediately. Then, in a whisper, she said, "Monsters."

Rachel's first instinct was to laugh, but the girl was so obviously serious that she was left more confused than anything else. If only her dad was there. Then, suddenly he was there, standing over them, looking down quizzically at Annie.

Before he could speak, though, another disturbance agitated the crowd. A knot of gray-clad men was pushing through the gathered onlookers toward them.

Because of all the people, Rachel hadn't seen them until they almost reached her family's now-surrounded picnic blanket.

Someone at the back of the little group was hollering, "Make way for the council. Make way!"

Then something else about the little group registered and Rachel let out a sound halfway between a laugh and a snort. "Daddy, are they wearing dresses?"

"Robes, Rachel." Paul sent her a quelling look and stepped forward to meet the little group. "Gentlemen?"

"Paul Casisia." The presumed leader, a severe man with an absolute proboscis of a nose, seemed less than pleased as he tromped the last yard or two through the grass to reach them.

The rest of the onlookers were spreading out, and, presumably because the crowd saw the planetary council, the noise level in the area had died down.

Paul nodded to the man with the huge nose, expression impassive. "Reuben Stegler."

The rest of the group straggled to a stop in a semicircle around Paul, with grim expressions up and down the line. Only one or two wore open, friendly looks. Stegler cleared his throat, eyeing the incongruous shape of Hope One sitting behind them, and asked, "You had to set down in the park?" He shook his head. "You realize, this won't make reinstating you any easier?"

Paul snorted. "I didn't come back to take up the governorship again, Reuben."

At this pronouncement, a sharp hiss of breath rippled across the gathered crowd and council alike.

Rachel's attention was divided between Annie, at her side, and the men talking over them. Annie was staring around again, wide-eyed.

"What monsters?" Jon whispered to her, keeping his voice as low as he could so as not to interrupt the conversation going on above.

Annie shook her head, obviously unable to put her fears into words. Then, the same bullhorn voice that had been shouting for the crowd to make way interrupted the adults' conversation above. "Paul, we need you." The speaker had actually gone pale, and he eyed the crowd around him as he continued. "Folks are on the verge of rioting. They want to destroy all the earth-tech. We can't keep the lid on it anymore." A murmur of agreement rose up from those surrounding them, and Paul looked around, startled.

The man seemed desperate now, and his voice was pleading as he stared Paul in the eye. "You're the only one who still has the authority to talk to them, Paul."

Paul frowned in concern, "Is it really that bad, Standish?"

Rachel was distracted by a *crunch* off to one side, from a distinctly open space. She turned her head to look, but there was nothing there.

Annie went rigid against her, and Rachel narrowed her eyes, reaching for Energematrice6. If there was something there, she would sense it through Energematrice6. Nothing could hide from those senses, and she *knew* she'd heard something. As the colors around her intensified and her awareness of everything stretched, Rachel caught a glimpse of something moving slowly and steadily across the open space.

At that moment, though, someone threw a rock at Hope One. It smacked into the vessel's side with a loud **bang** and Paul's head jerked toward the sound.

With an exclamation, her dad used Energematrice6 himself. Rachel was reasonably good at manipulating the powers that underlay all of creation, especially after being taught by her dad for the last ten Aterrian years, but Paul's skill was so great, she couldn't imagine how he did it. Instantly, invisible barriers sprung up between their little group and the surrounding crowd. Anyone who was too close was pushed bodily—though not roughly—backward and away. People scrambled to get clear of the invisible wall, as it steadily expanded. Some were obviously panicking, and Rachel lost track of whatever it was she had almost seen.

Soon, the little group consisting of the council, Paul, and the children had a clear space around them a hundred feet across. The same sort of strange barrier was simultaneously being erected around Hope, Rachel saw. When her dad got really irritated, he found interesting ways to show it.

Standish let out an exclamation, "By the void, Paul! That's *not* going to help!"

Paul snorted. "What do you suggest? Just let them damage our ship?"

Indeed, the crowd was murmuring aloud, though with Paul's barriers in the way they couldn't get at either the group or Hope. A few pounded fists against the invisible wall, but that was obviously futile.

Then Paul's voice rang out, amplified by even more weaves of Energematrice6. "People of Aterria, please give the council room for discussion. We intend you no harm..." he grimaced as another rock bounced off his barrier, "...but as of now, Hope One is off limits."

Stegler nodded sourly, his eyes sweeping the surrounding crowd. "You realize, setting Hope down in the middle of the park didn't help either. The more we remind them of the past...of where we came from...the worse they get."

Paul looked up at Hope with a thoughtful look on his face, but shook his head. "I didn't know, actually. When I left, there were a few murmurs, but it was nothing like this." He motioned to the press of people around them, a few of whom had resorted to beating futilely on the invisible ring around Hope in obvious frustration.

Standish spoke once more. "We know you believe there are still dangers from the outside, Paul, but without your help there may be nothing left on Aterria to protect. Without Earth tech, we won't even be able to grow food, and these people want to destroy everything!" He gesticulated at the crowd, which was milling about, with more people pushing away from the council now and toward Hope One. "They're calling Aterria the 'New Eden.'" He snorted derisively. "As if we could just go around picking fruit off the trees." He eyed the fruitless, evergreen-like trees down slope balefully as if it was somehow the trees' fault.

Rachel's concentration was interrupted once more as Annie stiffened and lifted a hand to point at the barrier off to their right. There was a gap in the crowd there, but Rachel still saw nothing, either using Energematrice6 or... wait. There *was* something there. What was it?

Even using Energematrice6, the whatever-it-was faded in and out of her vision. She couldn't see or sense it clearly. Then it smacked Paul's barrier and for a second she did see it clearly. It looked like a lumpy, misshapen child, but with gray skin and huge, black eyes.

Then it was gone again, and Rachel looked down at the girl clinging to her side. Monsters indeed. What *was* that thing?

"Shh," Rachel whispered to Annie. "As soon as Dad's done talking, I'll tell him. We're safe in here." She looked around at the barrier surrounding them and shivered. What was that thing? And what was it doing here?

"But Seebur!" Annie's frustration had overcome her timidity, but though she twisted back and forth, looking almost frantically for someone or something, she didn't rise from her place next to Rachel.

Rachel's attention, in turn, was pulled away once more by Paul's voice. "So you would have me become your king?" Paul's troubled glare raked across the council, oblivious to whatever-it-was that had become momentarily visible assaulting his barrier. He seemed almost horrified rather than angry. The council looked uncomfortable, but one man, stocky and bearded, actually nodded, while several of the others shrugged sheepishly.

Stegler sounded almost resigned. "*Something* has to be done. If not a king..." Stegler looked over at Standish, who had seemed about to speak, "...and no, I don't care what you call it, Standish. It's king we're talking about making him, whatever title you attach. If not a king, then what would you suggest, Paul?"

A sharp, mocking voice cut in. "And so you would make him king in deed, even if not word. Because whatever he suggests now, you will accept. Not without your grumbling —to make you feel important—but accept it you will. Ya fools." The new voice came from beyond the edge of the council, but inside Paul's barrier. Everyone turned to see who was speaking, and several members of the council let out low groans.

Annie, on the other hand, relaxed, and her attention fixed on this new speaker, as if she had finally found what she was looking for.

"Who asked you, Radding?" Stegler ground out between clenched teeth.

Paul snorted again, this time in amusement, and raised a hand in greeting. "Siever, it's good to see you. Can always count on you for a dose of honesty."

Siever Radding snorted in turn, his face twisted in disgust, but his eyes twinkled. "Not much good to be found around here, that's certain. ...Seeing you is an improvement, though." The admission was grudging, though he did send a smile in Paul's direction.

One of the council grumbled, "Why'd you have to let him in?"

Paul stared the man down, but before he could speak, Radding's glare once more assaulted the council and the twinkle in his eyes turned dark. "These fools strutting around in their brand new dresses, claiming they have the right to tell everybody what to do. What does 'Telestry' even *mean*, eh, Stegler?"

"Telestry?" Paul raised an eyebrow, looking around at the council, who shuffled sheepishly. A few folded their hands behind their backs to hide the lace edging the sleeves of their robes. That lace had to have come with them from Earth in someone's personal luggage. Aterria couldn't produce such things yet, certainly not in any quantity.

Stegler's mouth turned down at the corners in distaste, but he answered quickly enough. "It was all we could think of, Paul. The Telestry is an advisory council to consider the effects of Energematrice6 and technology upon the population as a whole. The robes were..."

"Your idea!" Radding smirked triumphantly.

"And you went along!" Stegler shot back. He shook his head in frustration and turned to face Paul squarely. "Even Siever was worried enough about the situation to join as a founding member of the council, Paul. This is deadly serious."

It was Radding's turn to look uncomfortable, and he nodded grudgingly. "Somebody had to keep an eye on you. I don't trust you, Stegler."

Stegler shook his head, exasperated, then looked back to Paul. "Something has to be done. You are the only hope we have left. The people are ready to destroy every scrap of technology we brought with us! Without Lastis or some other handy target, they're blaming Energematrice6 for what happened on Earth. Any technology we brought here is fair game. They've already started wrecking whatever they can lay their hands on."

"Luddites." The grumble came from somewhere in the knot of council members—they held the same sentiment.

Annie was pulling at Rachel's sleeve and pointing once more, and Rachel focused again to see—was that a hole? The monster, whatever it was, had apparently dug a hole under the edge of the barrier, and she looked over at it just in time to see it pop up under the barrier, a triumphant look on its ugly face before it started determinedly toward them, fading away once more.

Paul considered Stegler for a long moment, then asked, "If I told you five ships full of Lastis's goons were preparing to descend on Aterria, would that change anything?"

It was then that Rachel decided she had to do something to stop the creature herself. She stopped paying attention to the conversation and focused, creating a bubble of blue power, invisible to the naked eye, around the entire little cluster in the middle of Paul's larger clearing. Blue was her specialty, and it was perfect for stopping physical motion. Siever was only just inside the bubble, but it should be enough...

When she looked up, she caught a sharp glance from both Siever and Paul, but Stegler was still talking. "Are... Are you certain?" He seemed taken aback.

Paul sighed, once more giving the council his attention, "No. There's no indication of that yet." He shook his head. "But... There may be worse things out there even than Lastis Ralond."

As if on cue, the little monster bounced bodily off the shield Rachel had been constructing, becoming visible not just through Energematrice6, but to her physical eyes as well. It let out a snarl that sounded like it was gargling gravel and reared back to punch her shield with a fist that looked like a small boulder.

Paul and the council stared at it in shock, but Siever Radding must have noticed something before it actually reached the shield, because she felt his power reaching out to seize the thing.

Whatever it was sensed Siever's power before it coalesced fully, and it leapt straight at him.

Annie moved unexpectedly, and when Rachel looked down the little girl was up and running toward Siever. Rachel caught a scared, determined look on her face, then she passed through Rachel's bubble and, because she hadn't designed it to withstand impacts from the inside, the shield burst.

After that, everything happened at once. The monster, barely chest-high on Siever, lunged for him. Annie passed directly behind it and Rachel caught a flash of...something shiny...from the little girl's closed fist as she punched the monster in its back, as high as she could reach. Siever blasted the thing backward with a gout of Energematrice6. It flew through the space Annie had just been occupying as the little girl stopped short in her run and turned to grab around Siever's leg.

Rachel blinked, and Paul and the council came to life once more, breaking through their shock.

"What in *blazes*?"

"Voids! What *is* that?"

It was a good question. Now that the monster was stunned or dead, it was clearly visible. It had lumpy, gray skin that might have been made of rock or clay, based on the texture. The arms and legs seemed too long for its body, splayed out across the ground as they were. By far its most arresting feature was the eyes—huge, black, and almost flat. They stared lifelessly, for it was almost certainly dead, based on the green slime that coated its torso, oozing from a great gash in the middle of its lower back.

Rachel shot a look at Annie, still clinging to Siever's leg. Nobody inside the clearing besides her and Jon had been in a position to see what the little girl had done when she was behind it. What was that flash she'd seen? It could have been a knife, but how could such a small child effectively stab something like that? And Rachel would have sworn she'd had no knife before.

Paul held up a hand for calm, walking toward the strange creature, now collapsed on the ground in what could almost be mistaken for a heap of rock and gray mud. "Did you arrange that, old friend? As a demonstration?"

He looked at Siever Radding, somewhere between amused and curious. The crowd, meanwhile, was obviously confused. The entire incident had only taken perhaps three seconds, and even Rachel, who had been looking right at it the whole time, wasn't sure what she'd seen.

Siever laughed and shook his head, "Wasn't my doing." He shot a sharp glance down at the tiny girl still clinging to his leg.

The rest of the council paid Annie no mind at all, pointing at the thing and gabbling like geese. With a twinge of disgust, Rachel wondered what they would have done without Siever or Annie or even her. Died one by one probably, she thought.

"As you see." Paul addressed them sternly. "There are more things than we know lurking out in the darkness of space." Rachel snorted; Aterria was far from the darkness of space. Paul sent her a quelling look, though, and she held her tongue.

Radding, still standing several paces back from the council, let out a sharp laugh, "Even you haven't seen the worst of it yet, Paul."

Paul glanced over to Radding, his expression grave, and asked, "Why? What have you seen, old friend? ...Other than *that*, I mean."

Radding opened his mouth to answer, then seemed to think better of what he'd been about to say. Instead, he shook his head and grimaced as if from some sort of internal pain.

He looked Paul directly in the eye, and spoke. *"From the Void They Come; Beyond the Edge of The Real; Untouched by the Power of Creation; Inimical to Light."* Everyone knew Siever was some sort of mystic or prophet. Not many ever got to see exactly what that meant, however. His words, obviously some sort of prophetic utterance, had stilled the council.

Siever's hand rested on Annie's shoulder, and his attitude was once more that of a crotchety old man when he spoke again. "The situation here sucks, but they have no idea what you're fighting. Me... I've seen it." With that, Radding turned and pulled Annie a dozen paces off to one side, sitting down in the grass as she perched beside him.

Paul was staring at his friend when Stegler finally spoke, half strangled. "Well, if you must go, will you... will you at least advise us before you leave? Or speak to the people?"

He gestured at the surrounding crowd, now beginning to slowly disperse. Apparently, only the front ranks had seen what happened with the strange monster. Some few still stared transfixed at the odd lump on the grass.

Paul chuckled dryly, without humor, then nodded. "Give them what they want."

Stegler looked like a deer in the headlights of an oncoming vehicle. "But... But we'll starve!"

Paul shook his head. "You said the Telestry is 'a council to advise them on the effect of Energematrice6 and technology.' So advise them."

Stegler shook his head in turn. "We've told them the technology is necessary. They won't listen."

Paul closed his eyes and shook his head. "Not all of it. Let them destroy the Energematrice6 technology. Every one of you has the gene. You can use the power yourselves. Preserve the necessary tech—the old tech. Let the rest go." He scowled at them. "Now leave us in peace. We'll be outbound again after lunch."

Stegler thought over Paul's suggestion for a moment then nodded slowly. "I suppose...yes. We may be able to do that." He blinked. "If there were no E6 machines. If humans were only able to use Energematrice6...by their own power? What would the universe be like?"

Paul looked as if he'd bitten something sour—as if he *could* imagine what that might be like and didn't like it, but he shrugged. "Needs of the moment."

Then, Paul turned to the crowd and once more spoke through weaves of power that amplified his voice. "The council's deliberation is complete. Please return to your homes. They have reached a decision and will announce it to you within the day. I bid you farewell, people of Aterria."

One by one, the council paid their respects and turned to straggle away with the crowd. As they trudged down the hill, Paul spoke once more to their retreating backs, "I cannot be your king. I may, at best, be your advisor. At worst, a guardian against the darkness." He eyed the strange form, still laying on the grass.

Watching them walk down the hill, a little knot of gray robes among the rest of the crowd, Rachel asked, "What about Siever?"

Paul nodded and all three rose to walk over to the bent, crooked form of Siever Radding, staring into the distance from where he sat on the hillside next to the small girl.

She grinned up at Rachel as they approached. "Found Seebur!" She looked over at the strange corpse. "And a monster. I scared the others away, too!" Her obvious pride at this announcement left Paul frowning. Obviously he didn't understand the role she'd played in the little drama. Rachel wasn't sure she fully understood either, after seeing the gaping wound in the monster's back.

Siever smiled crookedly at Annie, fondness softening his craggy features.

Paul asked, "Are you alright, old friend?"

Siever shrugged. "It never touched me."

"What was it?" Paul's curiosity, never deeply buried, came to the fore.

"A monster!" Annie's delighted giggle brought involuntary smiles to everyone's faces. "And it doesn't like Emagematus. Seebur needs to be careful!"

Paul frowned, taking a moment to parse Annie's pronunciation of 'Energematrice6,' then raised an eyebrow at Siever in question.

"Golem." Siever's monosyllabic reply was disgusted, almost dismissive. At Paul's expectant silence, he sighed and added. "They *are* resistant to Energematrice6. She's right. ...And bloody hard to see unless they want to be."

Paul asked, "Should I stay?"

Siever laughed. "They mostly leave us alone. Took a disliking to me awhile back. She's right about that too." He glanced ruefully over at Annie, who turned to hug him tightly.

"What about her?" Paul asked.

Siever laughed, patting the little girl on the back. "Stray. Found 'er and took 'er in. We're good for each other."

Paul nodded, accepting the explanation without question. "Well, she needs to be careful. That thing could have hurt her."

"Yes, it could." Siever gave Annie a look, and Rachel couldn't help but see the layers of meaning in the statement. Her dad still had no idea that it was Annie rather than Siever who had dispatched the creature.

Rachel snorted, about to speak up and expose the little charade, but Annie gave her a conspiratorial grin and she thought better of it. A glance at Jon's expression confirmed her decision. He agreed. It wasn't their secret to tell.

Soon, Siever and Annie said their own goodbyes and headed off down the hill toward Casisia City, leaving Paul, Jon, and Rachel to continue their long-interrupted picnic.

It felt a little strange to simply sit back down and pick up where they'd left off, but Rachel found herself a bit amused as well.

After a few bites, she asked, "Why'd we come back anyway, Dad?"

Paul sighed, "I should say it was to check on them, but the real answer... I came back because I missed the sky. We weren't made for the void, and you shouldn't have to grow up in the darkness."

Rachel's reply came out far more grumpy than she'd intended, but it fit her mood. "Yeah, but dealing with people is complicated."

Paul chuckled and nodded, then smiled crookedly over at her. "Without other people, we'd go crazy. People are important, even if they are complicated."

Rachel snorted, "Shrewtongue is enough to drive me crazy all by herself."

Paul scowled at her, "I told you to leave Matilda alone, Rachel." Then, more gently, "She's just trying to help. Lightmaker knows we get little enough of that."

Rachel bit back a retort with some difficulty. Her dad deserved better from her than vented spleen. She wasn't really angry at him anyway. Paul was the best dad she could imagine, through everything that had happened to them. She didn't really know why she was angry. She had been since they left Earth, but it wasn't fair to aim it at her dad, however much she wanted to sometimes. Maybe the thought of having Annie as a little sister had set it off again, she thought.

They finished their lunch in silence, enjoying the cool, fresh breeze and the beauty of the world around them. Rachel's initial instinct to pout slowly subsided. She still didn't like Shrewtongue Mathison, but she couldn't help admitting to herself that her father had been right about the picnic. There was something about the blue of the sky and the emerald hues of the surrounding park that gave them a peace nothing in space could.

As they were packing up, Jon asked, "Are they going to have enough food, Dad?"

Paul considered a moment, then shrugged. "I know you were young when we landed." His mouth twisted in a wry acknowledgment of Jon's apparent lack of aging, but he continued without pausing. "When we first got here, there were plenty of plants, just nothing we could eat. We brought enough seed stock with us, though, that if they're careful they should be fine. All the Earth plants grow well enough here. If they use their resources right, basic Earth tech is enough to feed them."

It was with some reluctance that they re-entered Hope and lifted off once more into the skies of Aterria and from there to the blackness of space beyond. Paul, Jon and Rachel all sat in silence in Hope's command center until the Retton drive cut in, gravity returned, and Rachel asked, "So... We're going to the Redoubt."

Paul gave her a sidelong look and nodded briefly. Rachel sighed. "But why, Dad? We can't even work with the matter transistor properly there."

Paul frowned in thought for a moment before he answered. "You know how the Energematrice6 emissions from those stars are so strong?"

Rachel nodded impatiently. "That's what I'm talking about. It makes experimenting with E6 about twenty times harder."

Paul nodded in return, still thoughtful. "It's also where we came through from the Milky Way. It couldn't be designed better to hide a Retton drive. Could it?"

That particular line of thought obviously hadn't occurred to Jon before. He stared at Paul openly. "You're saying somebody called us there on purpose when we came from Earth? To give us cover?"

Paul gave him a tight smile. "Maybe. I remember..." He trailed off, his eyes far away, then changed the subject after a moment. "We're not the only ones it would hide though, are we."

It was silent in the command center for a long time, then Rachel asked quietly, "You really think Lastis is coming after us?"

This time, Paul's smile didn't reach his eyes. "When we escaped from Earth, we punched straight through the fabric of space. We were outside of everything that's real.

When we came here, we punched back through from... wherever that was. Anybody who thinks we didn't leave some kind of track is crazy... and..." He trailed off after a moment, seeming troubled.

"And what, Dad?" Jon asked, when it was clear that Paul wasn't going to continue.

"I'm worried it might be more like a funnel than just leaving a trace behind." He looked at them soberly. "I'm even more worried that if anybody else came through, it would warp even more."

It took a moment for both of them to digest Paul's statement, and Jon's reply was puzzled, almost dubious. "Dad, you remember what you said when we were watching that old Earth science fiction show the other day and they ripped a hole into 'subspace?'"

Paul grinned at him. "Yeah, I know. Everything's moving through space so fast that if it were actual damage to the 'fabric of space,' we'd leave it behind instantly. We can't even tell how fast we're really moving because there's no fixed reference point."

"So what then?" Rachel knew her skepticism was obvious, but she couldn't help it.

Paul grimaced, groping for the words he needed to express what he was thinking."What I'm trying to describe is more complicated than just a hole in space. It's more like a portal. When we came back through, however we got here, we created an "off ramp" back into reality that was anchored to whatever real things were around us. We shouldn't even have been able to get back at all, you realize? I tried twice before it ever worked. I could sense reality...everywhere...but we were caught on the other side, and I couldn't get us back. It was the Redoubt that I caught hold of, the third time I tried. The question is how...or who...” This time when Paul fell silent, neither Jon nor Rachel interrupted his thoughts.

Rachel Casisia and her brother Jon were the first of the "Odds," but they were not the only ones in the Aurora Galaxy. Soon after their confrontation with the mob on Aterria, the Casisias encountered another who aged as slowly as they did.

Later, after Paul disappeared, the episode survived only in the memories of the three young people. For personal reasons, Teron Galton never shared his own recollection.

For a millennia, the story was lost to history, leaving Galton's origin shrouded in mystery until it was finally recorded and passed down by Jon Casisia several thousand years after the fact.

From the Void

Year 4 NST – Aterria, Aurora Galaxy

Over the month that followed the incident at the park, as Hope One patrolled the dense, bright star cluster they had dubbed the Redoubt, Rachel thought back often to their picnic. In hindsight, she was glad her father had set down in the park. It was a time she would never forget. Despite her appreciation for the memory, Rachel preferred being out among the stars. While Jon seemed able to more-or-less fit in whenever they landed, she had never really related to others her age. Her *apparent* age. Subjectively, in terms of time she had experienced, she and Jon were both over twenty five. Biologically, she was still thirteen. She still looked and felt thirteen, and no doctor or scientist on Aterria understood why.

Rachel got tired of the sidelong glances and whispered comments about how she was 'odd.' Not that she left such comments unchallenged.

Normally, she and Jon were like appendages of each other, or two halves of a whole. Maybe it was because they were twins, or some combination of that and how much they'd been through, but they understood each other almost perfectly,   and their personalities were complementary... Except when Rachel felt left-out. It was one of the few things that really irked her. Somehow, Jon was just better at fitting in than she was.

Out among the stars, they spent most of their time learning how to use Energematrice6 and experimenting with its capabilities away from Aterria where they might cause serious damage.

They'd only gained the ability to access the power shortly before they escaped Earth. She still wasn't completely clear on the details, but she knew that her dad and Carl Winton—and Lastis Ralond—had a lot to do with it. She'd actually been twelve years old at the time, and nobody wanted to tell her what was really going on. Now, there was no prying anything out of her Dad about it at all, and everyone else seemed to think the past was dead, as Shrewtongue did.

As best as she could piece it together, soon after Energematrice6 was discovered, her dad and Carl Winton had learned that Lastis Ralond was planning to take over the world using the new energy source. She knew that in those early days it had all been mostly theoretical. She remembered her dad talking about it like people talked about physics or magic. Then, everything changed and he started acting like it was a real thing that he could reach out and touch. Rachel still wasn't sure how humans, and especially Lastis, had gained the ability to use Energematrice6 directly instead of through machines, as Paul first had. She knew the rest of the world, including herself and Jon, had gotten their own ability to use it after they got sick with 'the fever,' as her dad said, a modified version of scarlet fever. She thought her dad and Carl had something to do with that too, but Paul always changed the subject when she asked.

The thought made her even more grumpy. She didn't like not knowing things. Come to think of it, she hadn't asked Siever Radding, though. He would know, and if anybody in the universe would tell her it would be Siever!

However it happened, she and Jon had gained control of Energematrice6 shortly before they left Earth, during the Troubles. Being able to control it didn't mean they were able to use it effectively, though, the way their dad could. Rachel still wasn't sure how Paul had come by the ability to use Energematrice6 as well as he did. It was when she was about ten years old that he first saved both her and Jon with his own power, and that was before the Troubles or 'the fever.' That was really all she knew, and as usual, he wasn't talking.

Rachel snorted in annoyance. She had lost focus on her weave, and the threads of power she had been manipulating tangled incomprehensibly. She growled and threw the entire construct out through the wall of the command center into space beyond where it subsequently shredded itself into oblivion in a minor energy discharge that they left in their wake instantly as they hurtled through the void.

Jon looked over at her, one eyebrow raised, "Something wrong?"

Rachel shot him an annoyed look and shrugged, "Just distracted."

Jon nodded, knowingly, "Thinking about why we're here."

Rachel shrugged again, her eyes going automatically to her dad, sitting at the other end of the command center.

She wasn't sure why she didn't want him hearing their conversation, but for some reason, she didn't. "Doesn't matter," she muttered.

Jon turned to hold out his own current project toward her. It was a knot of green loops, interspersed with multicolored threads weaving in and out of the mess in a regular, though not easily predictable, pattern.

"What is it? It's obviously not for matter transition." Rachel's Energematrice6 senses traced the knot, which was at a low enough power that it was completely invisible to her eyes. The shape was unlike anything she would have imagined creating herself. Jon liked things that grew, whether plant or animal, and the difference between the twins was never more obvious to her than when he came up with an idea like this one. It obviously had an organic purpose, but she might as well try to read another language as attempt to understand what his weaves were for.

Jon's reply was interrupted by a blast of static from the command center speakers and the flickering of wavy lines across the main view screen.

Paul, sitting across the large room, focused on his own explorations, startled to full consciousness and stared wide-eyed for a long moment before he spoke. "That's a Bright Future signal. It passed the encryption check or it couldn't have triggered the comm!" He stared at Jon and Rachel. They both stared back, eyes wide, and Paul turned to speak into the microphone port at his console. "This is Paul Casisia on Hope One. Can you repeat?"

More static ripped out of the sound system, the bridge's main monitor fuzzed with even more lines, and Paul frowned, "It's weak. I can try to boost it, but..." He shook his head and both of his children sensed his will as he reached out into the fields of Energematrice6.

Rachel knew that Energematrice6 communication was at least conceptually similar to radio communication, just as the Energematrice6 fields paralleled electromagnetic fields in many ways. Complex waves of Energematrice6 were broadcast in every direction, and even the most tenuous signal could be boosted dramatically with very little effort. It was odd that their receiver, which was designed to boost signals all by itself, wasn't doing the job.

After a long moment, Paul let out a low whistle. "They're outside." More static buzzed around them, with no change in its volume.

"Outside?" Jon was obviously puzzled. "Like... out in space?"

Paul shook his head, grimly this time, "Outside of everything... Outside of reality, like we were when we were transported from the Milky Way here to Aurora. It's amazing the signal fell back to us at all. It's more evidence that my theory was right. Still, what if it's Carl... I'd never forgive myself if..." This time, when Paul reached out with Energematrice6, his eyes actually unfocused. Whatever he was doing required truly immense concentration, and when she realized what it was, Rachel actually gasped aloud. Jon looked at her strangely for a moment. Then he too realized what their father was doing, and they both stared at Paul, wide-eyed. He was trying to open up the hole in space he thought they must have created to get to the Redoubt. Just a little, perhaps, but what else could it be?

Another burst of static blared, this time loud enough to make them both set their teeth.

Paul's eyes refocused and he grinned triumphantly at them as intelligible sound finally came through and the image on the screen darkened. For a few seconds, the picture didn't really clear, but the strange waving lines of static resolved enough for them to see a face, first as a blur then more and more clearly as the signal improved. After about five seconds, Paul let out an exclamation of surprise when he recognized the man on the viewer. "Wayne?! Wayne Galton?"

"Paul Casisia." The other man's expression, dull with shock and...something else...morphed first to surprise then relief.

"How did you get here?" Paul asked. The picture was continuing to clear, and Rachel sucked in an involuntary breath as she realized what she was seeing in the back corner of the display, behind Galton's head. It was a body, obviously dead. Her father saw it at the same moment she did and he reached reflexively for the control that would shut off the screen. He hesitated before he reached it, however, his face hard, then let his hand drop back to his side.

"I could ask you the same, Paul. It's been a hot minute, by the Fates. Why, I haven't seen you since before the War." His tone capitalized the last word automatically, as if there had only ever been one, while Rachel knew that the fires of a great many wars had flamed up across the Earth before they left. Did that mean... Her thoughts were interrupted as Galton continued. "Listen, Paul, I need your help. They... They got my Callie." His head involuntarily turned toward the dead woman behind him; the screen had cleared enough to see that it was obviously a woman. Her face had an Asian look about it, with long dark hair and painted fingernails. Rachel hadn't seen painted fingernails in years. There hadn't been room for such luxuries aboard Hope during the Escape, and the colonists on Aterria hadn't re-developed reliable cosmetics yet.

The picture was clear enough now that Rachel could see the woman's lifeless eyes, staring blankly across the room behind Galton, who was obviously struggling to contain his emotion. He shook his head and glanced over his shoulder in the other direction. "They're not far behind me, Paul. Dominant's faster than they are, but even once I pull ahead, I can't seem to lose 'em, and they've got a deconstructor." Paul's expression went grim, and Galton nodded confirmation.

"How did they get a deconstructor?" Paul sounded half-strangled. "Did Lastis learn how to transist matter mechanically?!"

Galton laughed grimly, without humor. "That one's on Kyle. He had the last of the lot. He was going to set it to max and take out their whole flotilla. Best we can tell, a shade got 'im. Now *They* have it." He shook his head. "They used it to take out Lionel. They're all gone, Paul. Kyle, Win, Lionel... Now Callie. And on top of it all, the void-consumed Watcher won't leave us alone!" Rage shone from his eyes, but he glanced over his shoulder again to a sight they couldn't see, and focus, if not sanity, returned to him.

"I think you're still outside of..." Paul struggled with words for a moment, even raising his hands as if to describe something, then just shook his head. "...everything. You're still outside of reality, Wayne. I could try to pull you in...pull you to us, but we can't afford to endanger the colony. I don't have anything to offer you. We can't even defend ourselves effectively."

Galton stared for a moment. "My son, Teron." He glanced over his right shoulder once more and shook his head, completely determined, almost belligerent. "He's all I got left, Paul. Somebody's gotta take care of Teron." He stared hard at Paul across the Energematrice6 link.

Paul shook his head almost helplessly. "We can't."

Galton shook his head explosively. "There's no choice. None. You wanna kill him too!?"

Paul raised a hand, almost pleading. "But the colony. If we pull you in here, it will lead Them right to us. Space in this area is already damaged." He grimaced. "I may have to push your ship away just to keep you from falling back into reality on our heads. It's just us here. I'm the only defense these people have."

Galton swore, then raised his hands pleadingly, "Ya gotta help me, Paul! There's nobody else. If you take Teron, I'll turn 'n fight. I'll take 'em all with me, I swear to ya."

There was silence for a long, frozen moment, with Paul Casisia and Wayne Galton matching glares through screens on separate sides of a barrier that divided reality itself. Rachel couldn't help staring at the dead, sightless eyes of the poor woman in the corner behind Galton. She imagined her own mother, also dead since before she could remember, and for a moment she *felt* the horrible weight of the gut-wrenching decision that lay before Paul. She could see the side of his face, and by the set of his jaw, she could tell the moment he decided...and what he had decided.

In that moment, all of Rachel's resentment and anger toward her father boiled up, completely unbidden and unexpected.

Here he was, willing to sacrifice a little boy on the off chance that it *might* lead Lastis Ralond back to the colony.

All he cared about was the idea of other people. He didn't really care about the people around him. What about her and Jon? Why did they always have to take a back seat to his *other* responsibilities?

Suddenly this boy she had never met, this Teron, became a representation for Rachel of all the ways her dad had failed her. He was a precious, innocent human being, and he was going to die because her dad wouldn't save him.

Rachel's anger flamed hot as Paul's jaw worked, trying to get out words she knew he didn't want to say, and she nearly cried out, not because of that anger but because she saw the other side of his decision as well. She saw how the sacrifices he had made and the decisions that cost others lives had cut him so deeply, and though she was still angry and hurt, she loved her dad. She couldn't—*wouldn't* let her selfishness get in the way of that.

"What about a space suit?" She broke in, feeling desperation clawing at her, before her dad could speak and damn himself in his own eyes for the sake of the colony.

He turned his head to her, frowning, "What, Rach?"

"Does he have a space suit? We can pull Teron in. He doesn't have to drop his ship in at all. A space suit wouldn't be as bad as a whole ship... right?" A second later, very quietly, she added, "You can't do it, Dad. You can't!" She knew her eyes were pleading with him. She felt it from the bottom of her heart. If her dad turned this boy away, he would never be the same...and she saw Paul nod, first reluctantly, then more firmly, with his own relief.

"Wayne, if you can get him in a suit and out away from the ship, I'll pull him through to us." Paul hesitated, then added. "And you, too."

Galton laughed darkly, but he never even hesitated, "I'm already dead, Paul. Save Teron." He disappeared from the viewer without another word and Paul's mouth tightened.

"Where *are* they, dad?" Jon seemed befuddled. He'd obviously been doing his own exploration, trying to follow the Energematrice6 waves back to their source, Galton's vessel, without success. The communication signal was simply appearing in the void before them, and their own communication signal, while it didn't seem to disappear, was weakened far more than it should have been for the distance at which they were operating.

Paul shook his head, "I don't understand this any better than you do, son. I just know we can reach him."

It was a very long few minutes before Galton's face reappeared, but the three spent the time mostly in silence as their tension mounted. Finally, Galton poked his head back in front of the camera to demand, "Are you sure about this? Are you *sure* you can get him?"

Paul nodded without hesitation. "I'll get him, Wayne."

Galton's face disappeared once more and Paul closed his eyes, concentrating. Another long minute passed before Jon and Rachel saw his face tense and he seemed strained for a long moment, then he sighed and opened his eyes. Simultaneously, Rachel felt a strange sinking feeling in the pit of her stomach and a sensation of eyes staring at her from behind. It was so strong that she reflexively turned her head to see who—or what—was behind her...whatever it was, it absolutely *hated* her. Chills ran up and down her spine and she hunched forward, hugging her arms around herself.

It wasn't long before Galton returned once more to stare into the screen, his skin now gone pale. He didn't even have to ask the question that consumed him, it was so plainly written across his face.

Paul just nodded to him, then added, "We have to go pick him up, but he's here."

Galton's expression went slack with relief, then he changed the subject. "I'll take as many of 'em with me as I can, Paul. An' I'll get that deconstructor. I swear it on my my life."

Paul nodded once more. "Godspeed, Wayne Galton."

Galton returned his nod. "Take care of him." Then, his face disappeared and the screen went blank.

Rachel shivered again. The sensation of a hostile, completely evil gaze staring at her back hadn't gone away.

Paul immediately started Hope moving toward her new passenger, stranded in a space suit in the vastness of the emptiness at a location only Paul could properly pinpoint. Rachel rubbed her neck and looked around once more. No one had—or could—join them in the command center. They were the only people aboard Hope One, but she would have sworn there was someone staring at her, maybe in preparation for plunging a knife into her back?

She looked over at Jon, who met her eye and just nodded. He felt it too.

"Daddy?" Rachel began giving voice to both of their concerns. Paul looked over at her and gave his head a single, firm shake—No.

She cut off mid-thought, her mouth hanging open for a long moment, the gaze on her back making her feel anxious. For once, she didn't resent his command to be silent, probably because the eerie strangeness of that evil presence left her so alarmed.

Paul's own gaze was sharp but level and she just nodded back. It took two truly awful hours for them to find the lone space suit, floating in the void. Paul never relaxed, and he carefully began to guide the suit in as their autopilot matched trajectory with the drifting form, then approached slowly enough to avoid triggering the particle collision field that guarded the ship against micro-meteors.

Still, they waited in silence, all three using senses enhanced with Energematrice6 to watch the precious cargo approach. When finally their trajectories matched perfectly and the Retton drive cut out, Paul said simply, "Wait here, Rach. Watch the controls." Then, motioning for Jon to follow him, he pushed himself out of his chair and floated toward the hatch leading toward the airlock at the ship's base.

Rachel continued to keep her own invisible eyes on their new passenger through the hull of Hope as Paul and Jon pulled him into the airlock and proceeded to strip his suit from him. As she watched, Rachel used her console to lay in a new course, taking them back toward Aterria and, hopefully, safety. Because the others were moving in free-fall, she didn't dare start the autopilot, even if she desperately wanted to. The hostile presence still hadn't abated, and she could barely contain her impatience as she watched all three of the others slowly approaching through the passageways of the gravity-deprived ship.

When the three finally reached the command center, she was practically ready to jump out of her skin.

Paul immediately went to his customary console and strapped himself in, then looked over the autopilot program Rachel had already laid in. He hissed in alarm and immediately set to work changing it. Her protest died on her lips at another sharp glance, and she settled mutely in to wait. Jon, meanwhile, was strapping Teron into a console, then immediately returned to his own. Rachel noticed that he took the precaution of disabling Teron's console almost immediately.

The boy himself barely seemed to know where he was. He wasn't crying or complaining, though. If anything he was in shock. Jon noticed her curious glance and shrugged. "I sedated him a bit. He was...not doing well."

Rachel nodded, continuing to study the boy's face. He shared the Asian cast of his mother's features, and his wide, staring eyes might almost have matched his mother's dead ones. Rachel shivered again, for entirely different reasons than before and set to work scanning their surroundings. Doing something beat doing nothing with the invisible eyes never wavering from directly behind her.

After what felt like an age, they finally began to move. Rachel registered automatically that their speed was significantly higher than she would normally have expected.

Good.

Their direction, however, was at a significant tangent to the course they would have had to follow in order to return to Aterria. Rachel stole a glance at her father, then intentionally slowed her racing thoughts enough to figure out why he'd done it. It was obvious, really. If whatever was watching them... The Watcher, as Wayne Galton had called it, followed them back to the colony, that was a Very Bad Thing.

Even with their greater-than-usual speed, it took well over an hour for the strange sense of eyes on their backs to begin to abate. Rachel finally fell asleep when the sensation diminished enough to allow it.

Her dreams were dark enough to make her wish she hadn't slept at all. Ever since they reached the Aurora Galaxy, Rachel had dreams of Earth that she rarely remembered fully and didn't wish to remember at all. It was an Earth torn by war and destruction, a dark place where monsters walked the world and people were treated like animals.

These dreams were far worse. Earth became Aterria. The monsters hunted her friends—those few she still called friends in some way—and freedom was lost to humanity even here. Eventually the dreams faded, leaving her in a troubled doze.

She awoke an indeterminate time later, with her mouth tasting foul and her eyes burning. Across from her, next to Jon, Teron was apparently waking up as well.

She looked over to where her father still sat in his chair, stoic and determined, though the grimness in his eyes had diminished.

Most obviously of all, nothing remained of the strange sense of being watched. Her relief was instant and she allowed herself to bask in it for a few moments as she awakened fully. Then Teron spoke aloud for the first time, "Who are you?"

He was looking directly at Rachel rather than Jon, and she smiled tentatively in return. "I'm Rachel."

"I'm Teron."

"I've always wanted a little brother, Teron." Rachel met his gaze levelly. She didn't smile. This boy had been through too much. She could see it in his eyes. He didn't need someone to jolly him along. He needed someone to take him seriously.

Teron looked sad, "I've never had a sister." He looked at Jon. "Or a brother." He didn't look at Paul at all, and Rachel could see the pain behind the boy's eyes. She simply nodded in return.

It was then, with Teron Galton staring at her, that the full emotional impact of what had happened actually came home to her. This poor little boy would never have his mother or father ever again. His situation was just like hers—given time, he would feel just like she had been feeling for a very long time—but far worse. After all, she still had her daddy, and he was a good man—the best.

In that moment, Rachel's resentment melted away and the next thing she knew she had unbuckled from her console and was all the way across the command center with her arms wrapped around her dad. She hugged him as tight as she could with her thirteen-year-old muscles that refused to mature, and absolutely bawled her heart out.

Belatedly, it occurred to her that something most definitely *had* found them now and it was because of her idea to bring a boy she had never met aboard. It was her fault.

She didn't care. Teron was worth it.

When her tears finally abated, it was to the sound of Teron's voice addressing Jon in a befuddled tone. "Girls are weird."

Jon's resulting laughter was mischievous and free, and as her dad began to chuckle Rachel gave Jon the stink eye.

"Gee, thanks," she grumbled. It was a lame retort, but she just wasn't feeling very snarky at the moment.

Between the mysterious disappearance of Paul Casisia and the arrival of the Brightstar in the Aurora Galaxy was the time of Teron Galton, the Keeper of the Mysteries.

Galton faced many challenges and though he was never able to defeat the enemies that threatened humanity decisively, his tireless efforts created a safe haven for the people of the Aurora Galaxy and specifically the Telestry.

The Keeper of the Mysteries

Year 2220 NST – The Void, Aurora Galaxy

You should not have come here.

The tone of the thought was gloating and unmistakable. It grated on his mind.

For what must have been the millionth time, Teron Galton gritted his teeth, wishing it was easier to tell the difference between his own thoughts and the counterfeit nastiness The Watcher slipped into his brain. If he hadn't been so familiar with that ugly feeling, he would have assumed it was his own. It certainly carried his own sentiments this time. He *shouldn't* have come here...but he had.

On the plot stretching across the entire forward wall of the bridge, the amber star representing the Telestry's vessel winked insultingly in front of them. They had only just crossed into The Watcher's territory, which in his own mind marked the edge of the Abyss. Teron double checked their coordinates. The malevolent presence's area of influence had expanded yet again.

It calls to me. I WILL have it.

Teron grimaced. At least it wasn't trying to fool him into thinking its voice *was* his own thoughts anymore. That concession had only taken what? Almost a thousand years Earth time? He was grimly certain it was only because the malevolent entity had decided this open prodding was more effective. Teron felt oddly proud at the thought. He'd take any win he could get against this particular horror.

At this particular moment, The Watcher wasn't his biggest problem. That honor belonged to the Telestry, the most bullheaded of the galaxy's human powers.

"Lord Keeper! They're still on course for the Casisias' crystal; are you certain you want to keep pace with them? I'm getting..." Issachar had his face twisted into an expression Teron would normally have called unbecoming in an officer, and his oldest living friend, who was also Malak's captain, turned his head almost reflexively to see if someone was staring at him from behind.

Teron sighed, "Yes, Issachar. I feel The Watcher. I know we must look to the safety of the Sigil, but Jon and Rachel are in that crystal. Paul Casisia loved them. He would never forgive me if I allowed the Telestry to harm them. Take heart. The Watcher cannot do anything to us unless we allow it to break us. Guard your thoughts."

Issachar's face became an iron mask and he nodded, "Of course, my lord." Teron could see the grim determination in his friend's expression, much as he tried to hide his emotions behind his Regalian stoicism. Issachar was a good man—the best he'd known since Paul Casisia disappeared.

Every trip into the Abyss was a risk Teron couldn't afford. Even now, he knew The Watcher was pressing on the thoughts of every single member of his crew, trying to worm itself into their minds, tempting them to do something terrible, driving them insane. He had given

44

orders that no crewman was to be alone with their minds under assault. With distant curiosity, Teron wondered if the Telestry crew even so much as felt The Watcher's gaze on the back of their necks the way his own people did. He knew the Telestry was doing The Watcher's own work for it. Whatever meddling they planned to try on the crystal this time was beyond him, but if there was even a chance they might succeed, he had no choice but to follow them.

"My lord, we've received a hail from the Telestry. It's the vessel Ocharist... It's Drake Loriden, my lord."

Teron didn't allow his expression to change, but internally he cursed as The Watcher's gloating laugh boomed through the back of his mind.

"Put him on, Issachar."

"Here, my lord?"

Teron laughed mirthlessly, "If he's calling me in the Abyss, he knows we're not speaking privately." In response, Drake Loriden's dark, brooding visage appeared on the screen, replacing the master plot. For a long moment, Loriden didn't speak, obviously studying Teron.

Then, Loriden's eyes narrowed. "What business have you here, Keeper of the Mysteries?" He was obviously putting on more of an act than he needed to, probably because Teron hadn't taken his comm privately. Teron had known Loriden for four hundred earth years, more than a hundred and fifty years, New Standard Time. Loriden was something of a showman, enough so that it was easy to forget how effective an operative he could be. He didn't bother with his act in front of Teron anymore, but with anyone else present he couldn't seem to help himself.

Teron frowned at Loriden. "The Casisias are my charge, Telestic Loriden. I cannot allow them to come to harm."

Loriden smiled almost convincingly, an affectation Teron knew had no purpose beyond provoking him. "Why, then, have you not freed them from their imprisonment?"

On top of the irritation induced by The Watcher, the provocation worked. It was all Teron could do to keep his face smooth. "The time is coming, Loriden. I may not be able to free them, but Brightstar will. I am as nothing in *his* shadow."

Loriden's sneer was somehow even worse than the smile had been. "Yes. Your precious 'Brightstar.' How long have you been waiting, Galton? A thousand years?" He laughed, though Teron could tell there was no real mirth in Loriden either. The Abyss was the furthest thing in the galaxy from a joke and they both knew it, however Loriden might playact. After a moment, Loriden continued, "Don't worry, Keeper. When the Brightstar appears, the Telestry will do its part. You shall have your audience, even if we must stand to your defense. Malleus' wish will be fulfilled— if Brightstar ever comes." Loriden stopped, as if inviting him to speak, but Teron just stared grimly into the video pickup, waiting. Loriden liked to talk, and he was the one who had initiated the call, after all.

After another long pause, Loriden scowled. "If we should free the Casisias, you will have your audience with them as well. Even if the Brightstar is not present. Don't try my patience. This will be... delicate."

Teron ground his teeth. "You know the prophecies, Loriden. The Casisias may not—must not—be freed until Brightstar comes."

"Prophecies are chancy, Keeper. Our reading of the texts is...somewhat different. We will reach the crystal within the day. Unless you wish to incur the wrath of the

Telestry, stand clear. The ancient pact between us stands. You must not interfere." With that, Loriden cut the connection.

As the seconds passed in the aftermath of Loriden's words, Issachar made no comment. The rest of the half dozen or so bridge crew was too well disciplined to speak without leave. For his part, Teron was seething, but again he didn't show it. With The Watcher's relentless assault, his people were dealing with enough. His doubts must remain his own.

And doubts he had. Even Loriden, with his centuries-long lifespan, was but a child compared to Teron. He *had* been waiting for the Brightstar for a thousand years NST. That was three thousand years Earth time, which was similar to that of Aterria, home of the Telestry. Most of the people of the Aurora galaxy still aged at the same rate they always had, though some did live to be forty standard years old now—a hundred and twenty by Earth reckoning. He was the only one who remembered Earth anymore, and had been for a very long time.

Teron was still in his prime, though he didn't know how that was possible. The older he got, the less he was certain of. Why did he age so slowly? What of Loriden or the other 'Odds' as they were now so quaintly called? Time twisted all things. The 'ancient pact' Loriden had spoken of had originally been nothing more than Paul Casisia's annoyed admonition to the Telestry to 'mind what Teron told them and make sure to take the Brightstar to the Vale.' Teron snorted in disgust. Paul's peevish instruction had gradually decayed in the Telestry's consciousness from a general command to obey into no more than a grudging allowance that he got to have an 'audience' once the

Brightstar did finally show.

His part in the 'ancient pact' had never been specified, and he'd allowed the Telestry's fealty to Paul, to himself and to the Tenets to decay too far...not that their reverence of Paul had ever gone beyond lip service for more than a generation or two at a time. Malleus had been a breath of fresh air, but since Malleus, it had decayed beyond even lip service.

Teron knew he should have done something to bring them into line, but he didn't know what. The Telestry was completely unmanageable, and he was constantly occupied putting out some fire or other. As busy as he was dealing with the Ilvayn, the Opterans, the Nosufer or any of Their other, less organized minions, he always had some emergency to chase. He barely had time to think about the Dominion, the Telestry or the other human polities.

Whatever the cause, Teron had allowed the Telestry to become a problem, and short of invading Aterria and taking command of the unruly Energematrists by force, he had little recourse but to 'play nice' with what seemed to him troublesome children. He had seriously considered conquering them. Any of their Energematrists...or even all at once would be hard pressed to overcome the power of the Sigil of Mysteries, but what was he going to do? Kill them all?

Yes. Kill them ALL.

The Watcher's invasion of his mind had never really gone away, and its taunt was a pointed reminder of where they were and the cost of letting his thoughts run amok.

Teron sighed and turned to Issachar, "I will be in my quarters, old friend. Remember, Watcher protocols are in effect. Nobody goes anywhere alone. Double confirmation on every command decision." Issachar nodded at the order, redundant as it was. They all needed some redundancy in this place.

Teron turned to leave, doing everything he could to prepare himself mentally for what he knew would be a long, difficult wait.

Three days later, Teron's tension had built so high that he was internally ready to exercise the conquest option on at least the little piece of the Telestry represented by Ocharist. He stared at the image of the Telestry vessel on Malak's view screen, the Casisias' crystal in its primary cargo hold, with his jaw clamped shut so hard it ached. It had taken all the self-discipline he could muster to keep The Watcher at bay, first as Malak shadowed Ocharist on its approach to the crystal with the Casisias entrapped in it, then while they attempted to do something—he still didn't know what—to the crystal itself. Malak's crew was showing the strain as well. Twice already, crew members had tried to harm themselves, and The Watcher's malevolent presence was still intensifying. Both times, the two-together rule had saved them, but it was only a matter of time before someone dove out an airlock—or worse, into one of the emitter coils.

Issachar's determination also seemed only to have increased, and Teron was glad he wouldn't have to worry about his friend this time. The last time they had been in the Abyss...

His thoughts were interrupted by a loud exclamation from the technician at the sensor suite, but before Teron could speak Issachar was already moving. "What? What is it?!"

The technician turned toward Issachar, his expression confused. "I don't know, captain! There's something off the port bow...I think." He shook his head as if bewildered.

"Well, what is it? Get it on the viewer!" Issachar was nearly beside himself, and Teron could hardly blame him. Perhaps this was nothing, but at least it was a distraction from the constant creeping malevolence in their heads.

Do you REALLY think so?

Gloating laughter echoed through his mind as Malak lurched horribly.

The main view screen changed then, to show a strange shape, only visible in the Abyss's blackness because portions of it glowed slightly. Teron was already reaching for Energematrice6, automatically using the Sigil of Mysteries around his neck as an amplifier. Teron had been using Energematrice6 for literally thousands of years. Though the colors in the room around him abruptly intensified and he could clearly sense every object and even every molecule if he chose, his focus was so practiced and automatic that he barely noticed.

Teron's attention was already outside of Malak, using his Energematrice6 sense to search for their foe. It wasn't quite like normal sight. Instead, he could sense the space and every molecule that occupied it—not many out here. Whatever the enemy was, it had launched some kind of projectile at them, and Teron distantly sensed a giant crater on one side of his vessel. Subconsciously baring his teeth, Teron pushed his perception out into the void, looking for anything at all. Another incoming projectile streaked through his perception and with Energematrice6-boosted senses it was like a tracer, pointing him straight at his target—was that from some sort of rail gun? It had been moving blindingly fast.

When projectiles were propelled up near the speed of light, as the one that had hit Malak was, even a tiny object, the size of Teron's fist, could tear through the entire vessel like a bullet through tissue paper. Malak had Energematrice6 shields to protect it from such objects, but whatever the projectile was, it had exploded on impact. The energy released was so high that the weapons might as well have had nuclear warheads. Some of that was from the velocity, but it couldn't all have been so. Malak could only take so many hits like that one. Malak lurched around him again, but Teron barely noticed. He had found the enemy.

Without stopping to properly look at the vessel before him, Teron lashed out. His Energematrice6 specialization was Pyric, but all that meant at his level of mastery was that he reached for it out of habit whenever there was no reason to do otherwise. The gout of pure, plasmic energy that Teron released against his target was enough to consume ten ships like Malak. His white-hot fury at being attacked on top of the pent-up frustration and tension that had inexorably grown as The Watcher tormented him and his crew combined into what he knew must be overkill. Nothing in *this* galaxy could stand up against the power he had just unleashed. It was cathartic. This unknown thing had hurt his ship and probably killed people aboard Malak he had known since they were children.

The eruption of power flowed around him and through the void, coalescing into a lance of fire almost as large as Malak itself as it reached the enemy vessel to consume it.

Or at least, it should have. Instead, the blast wave of power flowed around the unknown enemy, rolling off as if magnetically repelled to streak into the void beyond.

Laughter boomed through Teron, almost breaking his hold on Energematrice6 as his mind was frozen, brittle with shock.

What had just happened was impossible. Everything in the universe was made from Energematrice6. It was the power that underlay existence! How could this be?

I WILL have the Sigil! I will take it from your corpse—from the wreckage of your precious Malak!

Real fear wormed into Teron's guts as the ship around him rocked yet again. Again he lashed out against the enemy, suppressed panic galvanizing him. Again, his gout of power streamed away, blue-white this time, only to wash over the other vessel without effect while return fire rocked Malak.

Alarms were sounding now, and Teron flailed with his power, trying over and over to land a blow while the enemy's attacks continued to roll in, and Teron felt despair gripping him. Grimly, he understood what would be required to defeat this foe. For reasons he could not understand, Energematrice6 would not touch it. He needed physical projectiles, but this far out into the Abyss there wasn't so much as space dust for him to lay hold of. Creating a physical object with Energematrice6 that was large enough to damage that strange vessel was impossible. The entropic shock would kill him if he tried.

Vaguely, as if from a world away, Teron heard Issachar saying something. "Loriden..." Teron struggled to focus enough to catch what his old friend was trying to tell him.

"...the Casisias."

"What?" Teron blinked stupidly up at Issachar.

"Loriden is taking the Casisias. They're free."

Another blow, even more severe, slammed into Malak as Teron stared at Issachar in disbelief. "That is impossible." They flinched as The Watcher's laughter boomed through both of them at the same time. Teron sagged in his seat as the blows abruptly stopped coming and The Watcher's voice returned with even more force.

Too long you defied me. No more.

The gloating tone consumed Teron's world.

Through his Energematrice6-enhanced senses, still spread like a net around Malak's ruptured, hemorrhaging hull, Teron sensed the enemy turning. On the screen before them, the vessel pivoted, its angles somehow wrong, as if their geometry had come from a completely different place, where reality itself was alien.

Then, the enemy vessel released a projectile four times the size of anything that had so far battered his beleaguered ship. Even through Energematrice6, he barely caught a glimpse of it as it streaked in to rip a hole completely through Malak, from one side to the other.

DIE, KEEPER.

Unshakable certainty gripped Teron. He felt as if he might as well be dead even before the final projectiles ripped out of the enemy vessel. It was as if he could feel them coming, even before they launched, and nothing could stop it.

But something did.

An object, barely bigger than a man, appeared from the depths of the Abyss, far beyond the enemy, moving even faster than the enemy's projectiles, which had been at close to light speed when they struck Malak. The object shone with Energematrice6, so charged with power it would have blinded him if it actually emitted photons. To hold a charge like that, it must be some kind of crystal. It was much larger than the projectiles the enemy had shot at Malak, but compared to a space vessel it was still impossibly small. How could it mount a drive capable of creating the Energematrice6 distortion for super-luminal travel? Nothing that small could possibly move so fast. The blows Malak had taken were terrible, but nothing Teron had ever heard of could propel a small object *above* the speed of light. That was why projectile weapons were so rare now. Whatever this was, it was moving many times faster than it should have been able to.

Teron's conception of reality took yet another blow as the object actually smashed into the enemy's vessel at an incalculable velocity.

The impact energy was so immense that Teron had trouble understanding what he watched. It wasn't even an explosion at first. Instead, the enemy vessel simply vaporized where the crystal had passed through it, going from a physical state to an energy state instantaneously. Then, well behind where the crystal had struck, the atomic energy it released consumed the rest of the vessel in a tremendous explosion.

Out of the fireball, a man-sized object, now reduced to a speed barely two or three times that of light, streaked across Teron's perception, as if following Ocharist and the Casisias. The screen in front of Teron was only just registering the enemy's destruction as the little crystal disappeared out of Teron's perception once more.

AAAWWWAAAAAAAAAAAAA!!!!

The Watcher's howl of inarticulate rage was awful, but the pressure it had been holding against Teron's mind suddenly, finally slackened as its champion was destroyed.

Issachar grunted. "Took you long enough."

Teron simply stared at him, his mind reeling. Then, understanding bloomed fully within him and he laughed, true mirth and joy rolling freely out of him for the first time he could remember.

Teron clapped Issachar on the shoulder. "*That* was not me. In fact…" He grinned. "*That* was the Brightstar! *Follow that crystal!*"

During the time of the Brightstar, at the height of the conflict, a strange new presence arrived in the Aurora Galaxy.

Tom Nelion's fame would never rival that of the Brightstar, but he played a role that would dramatically change the course of history.

His alliance with the 'Odds' who followed Nate Brightstar would eventually become the stuff of legend.

The Boy from the Darkness

Year 2222 NST – The Void, Aurora Galaxy

Tom Nelion had an Ikhu dancing on his last nerve. The thought made him smile sourly, even though it was almost literally true. The ancestor spirits had refused to leave him alone for weeks, even for a moment. They strained to possess his consciousness, and while his resolve and rejection of them had never slackened, their incessant whispers disturbed his calm. They kept him from thinking clearly, but they were his ancestors and he couldn't rid himself of them. There was little he could do but push forward toward his goal despite them.

His strange odyssey had finally brought him to what he hoped would be the end of his self-imposed quest. He finally stood on the soil of Aterria, the planet of the Telestics, who had been the Enemy of his people since before their history was recorded. Their conflict stretched back to an entirely different galaxy and a time the Telestics themselves had now forgotten.

Tom's bemusement and a sense of surreal disconnection from his surroundings carried him from the spaceport into the city proper, then onward toward the spires of the Telestry. The fact that he was alone here left him feeling naked and vulnerable, but so far it seemed his ancient 'enemies' didn't even know who or what he was.

There was no disguising his stature or his face. Some tribes of The People might pass for human if they tried—if their pride would allow such a degradation. Tom's long, sensitive ears and pronounced snout-like nose and jaw made such a task impossible for him. His pupil-less, electric blue eyes, far larger for his face than the humans' were in theirs, would have been difficult to disguise as well. The fine fur covering his face and neck put the capstone on a noble visage that was closer to an animal's than one of his distant, human cousins. Even his flesh, composed of crystalline matrix, was different from that of the humans.

All that aside, even making an attempt to appear human would have been a dishonor upon The People, so he simply forged ahead, ignoring the open stares and occasional flickers of fear in the eyes of passers-by.

It was reminiscent of what had happened in Bounty City, though in that instance the shock of being dropped into a world so unlike anything he had ever known was so strong he had acted... unwisely. Now he'd had a little time to get accustomed to this strange galaxy—a galaxy dominated by humans who lived freely and openly where neither the Changed nor The People nor any other denizen of the Dream would molest them.

He still didn't really understand how such a state was possible. How could these humans still be safe? Was it simple distance? Could those who walked the Dream not know of this place? Or was there more to it? He could still touch the Dream here, so he knew it had to be accessible to them... though it was different—brighter somehow.

Tom was caught mid-thought as a colorful creature covered in something that wasn't quite fur passed in front of him, diving through the air. Tom reflexively reached out, grabbing at the thing as it soared away, disappearing behind a tree. He caught nothing except a single piece of the creature's...body covering?

Tom had never seen anything quite like the long, flat... brush?...with its delicate, brightly-colored design. He had spent so little time on planets that he didn't even know what to call the winged, fluffy creature. Its beauty was remarkable, as was the rest of the world. Nothing he had known before had prepared him for the azure of the sky above or the radiant green of the leaves that rustled in the wind as he passed.

These humans had no idea how extraordinarily blessed their lives were, to exist in such a place. The architecture was beautiful as well. The spires surrounding Tom and to either side were graceful, yet solid and ancient.

Tom's musings ended abruptly when he found himself in front of gates seemingly made of light, set in a wall that stretched practically as far as he could see in both directions. His view of the wall's length would have been blocked if he didn't naturally see the energy of life that infused it, even through the buildings that rose before it, to either side of him.

Tom stepped closer to the gates, marveling. The complexity of the energy that wove through them was unlike anything he'd ever seen. Even Megalith hadn't come close to the workmanship of this ward surrounding the Telestry. Tom was tempted to simply absorb the Energy and punch through the gate, as was The Peoples' way, but what a shame it would be! Destroying such a work of art would be a crime.

Instead, Tom stopped to consider the barrier carefully, looking for another way through. He followed the individual strands of the weave, trying to puzzle out what each was intended to do. It quickly became impossible, but in trying Tom saw something else that sent a chill up his spine.

Tiny, hair-thin filaments of power ran down from the wall of energy into the ground beneath him. It ran far, far beneath him, and when he finally reached its termination, he withdrew his perception to stare at the shining edifice, thankful that he hadn't triggered that particular trap.

It was a clever ruse. If he had simply begun to draw power out of the wall, it would have worked. The life energy that flowed through the wall also supported the ground beneath his feet. If he had been foolish enough to disrupt those flows, he would have opened a well all the way down to where the world was molten, creating an explosive volcanic eruption, consuming himself and everything around him... except, of course, the gate itself. It was almost as if the profound beauty of the architecture surrounding him was designed to draw attention away from the deceptively boring ground beneath.

Tom chuckled darkly, his respect for the humans of this Telestry ratcheting up several more notches. Then, he sank down to the pavement before the Telestry, allowing his focus to flow more fully into his examination of the wall and its so-far impassable gate.

Tom became so engrossed in his task that time escaped him, flowing past like water down a drain. When the gate swung open, it wasn't due to any action of his. Instead, it simply opened, pulling Tom from the near Fugue state he'd sunk into and bringing him to full alert. The planet had rotated significantly, he found, and the system's star was no longer directly above him, instead hugging the horizon in preparation for the time of darkness. He must have been there for hours. The only real surprise was that in that whole time no one had come through the gate and woken him.

For a long moment, Tom hesitated, staring through the opening. Gates, and especially this gate, did not simply open of their own accord... Still, this was why he'd come. Pushing his wariness aside, Tom stepped forward through the gate and began walking once more.

The scenery inside the walls of the Telestry was much the same as outside—the same buildings and trees, though the spires inside were already taller than those without.

Tom's awareness of his surroundings never slackened as he walked, but he couldn't help but focus his attention on the sky. It was so different here, on the surface of the planet. The stars were faint and dim, all except one that was, he thought, not really a star at all. It seemed red to him, as if evil emanated from it, staining the sky around it with a ruddy haze. In the part of his awareness that extended into the Dream, Tom could see that there was something very wrong with that crimson point of light, but before he could ponder further his full attention was pulled back to the path before him.

Directly ahead, the path Tom was following branched, with forks to both the left and the right, and he smiled to himself. A group of humans was waiting for him around that corner—both corners. He could see their distinctive swirls of Energy through the walls of the buildings to either side, even though the walls, too, were fortified with the Energy.

Tom growled deep in his throat and felt his blood heat.

Ambush!

Setting his jaw, he took a firm hold on the instinct that urged him to jump forward into the intersection and rip the Energy from every one of those waiting figures. Recklessness had cost him enough. He gritted his teeth and looked longingly ahead for a moment—he'd hoped he would be able to see the plaza at the center of this magnificent place. It rivaled even the great works of the Old Ones, the first of The People, in its majesty.

Tom stopped in front of the intersection, just beyond the reach of those who awaited him. The Ikhu swirled and screamed their whispers in his ears, more agitated than he'd seen them since... the Bright One. Tom smiled grimly to himself and waited for his ambushers in turn, curious to see what these feral humans would do when they encountered one of The People.

It took several minutes before the first human cautiously poked his head around the corner, saw Tom, and jerked it back. There followed a whispered conference that Tom could hear even over the continued harassment from the Ikhu. Still ignoring the incorporeal beings and trying to hear the humans' whispers, Tom couldn't help smiling ironically to himself. The strength of the Telestics' Energematrice6 shields ranged from moderate to pathetic —contemptible even. None were even close to the strength of Tom's own shield. If he actually wanted to harm these humans, they would have been dead before they knew he was there. ...That could still happen, of course, but it wasn't what he'd come for.

A moment later, both groups of humans slowly began to emerge into the intersection from the branching paths to either side to stand before him. It took a few breaths for one to step reluctantly forward to stand in front of the others, staring sternly up into Tom's face.

"What do you want with us, Vampyr?" Her face was stoic, her words crisp, but Tom could smell the fear rolling off of her.

Tom nodded to her. He had no particular respect for humans, even those of the Telestry, but neither did he have any desire to provoke them. He had come to ask a question, not to fight. So he simply shrugged and asked her. "Where is the Bright One? I have come to speak with he who was sent by the Lightmaker."

The group's reactions to Tom's question varied dramatically. The woman before him never wavered, nor, he noticed, did the fear smell abate. If anything...it thickened? What could that mean? Her answer, too, was as firm and crisp as before. "There is none such among us, Vampyr. We cannot help you."

It was what some of the other Telestics did that made Tom's eyes narrow. When Tom mentioned the Bright One, a few of them reflexively looked up to the sky for a moment, at the tiny red not-star he had been contemplating earlier. It was only a flicker before their gazes returned to him, but enough of them showed the exact same response to leave Tom with little doubt of its meaning. Something was bothering him, however. The

Ikhu's screeches and jabbers had faded too much. They were positively subdued. Something was wrong.

Tom studied the speaker, his anger rising once more. She knew something. Again, he gritted his teeth and resettled his grip on his temper. "Yet you know where he is—that is plain. Why would you not tell me?"

Again, her answer made his anger spike, "Brightstar has enough trouble, Vampyr. I would not send him more."

Tom allowed a note of warning to creep into his tone. "I wish him no ill, human of the Telestry. However, I *must* see him. You *will* tell me where he is." If these Telestics wished to test him, they would find him ready for a fight. It might even appease the Ikhu for a time. He flexed his arms and widened his stance in preparation to move. The Ikhu gabbled in excitement and...

Unbidden, the memory of **her** face swam into his vision and his anger was gone as if it had been cut from him with a blade. Killing humans had a cost, whatever the rest of The People thought.

The Telestic shook her head and was about to answer once more when one of the others stepped forward, preempting her. The move caught Tom by surprise, but not as much as this human's aura did. That aura was black as night...as dark as... *Abyssal void*!!

Tom physically startled, jumping backward—something he'd seen humans do, but had himself never experienced. How could Tom have failed to notice one of the Taken? Humans inhabited by a denizen of the Dream were rare and dangerous. Was this Nightmare of the Dream world so much stronger than the one on Bounty that it could hide itself, not just from these humans but from one of The People? Tom focused his attention on the

Dream, still seeing nothing at first. His eyes snapped past the Nightmare riding the man, but when he focused now, he could sense that his perception was being manipulated as his vision slid away once more.

Tom tried again. When he finally saw the being, he almost cowered. It was enormous and so utterly light-consuming that seeing it darkened the Dream and even the world around him until he could make out little else.

Then the creature spoke, its voice coming with a curious duality, both in the physical realm through its human puppet and in the Dream, where it echoed around and through him, every syllable making the crystal of his matrix quiver. "What do you wish of the Brightstar, Nosufer?"

Tom stared at the Taken, his mind racing. He noticed with a corner of his attention that the woman who had first spoken was eyeing the Taken with annoyance.

Annoyance! Humans could be so stupid. She should be groveling before this being.

Apparently, Tom could be stupid too. He should have said something—anything—to distract the being. Instead, he was still staring at the Taken a moment later when the Nightmare calculated why he was seeking the Bright One... correctly, it seemed.

The Archon laughed at him.

Tom had only seen Nightmares on a few occasions, and never before an Archon—one who must be a ruler of the Dream. Always before, until Bounty, it had been from a great distance—which wasn't to say a safe distance. He had never seen one amused. The human meat puppet's laughter was again echoed in the Dream in a quivering symphony of dissonance, and after a moment the creature spoke once more. "Your kind aren't welcome in the Lightmaker's court, Nosufer. You were conceived in darkness just as all your kind were, millennia ago." The being's human face, obviously no more than a ghastly vessel, smirked at Tom.

Tom's eyes were drawn like magnets to the burning dot in the sky above them where he now knew the Bright One must be. "He didn't seem to think so." He felt a wistful tug on his memory along with the sinking dread that came from knowing how this encounter must end.

Tom resolutely returned his gaze to the Taken, his eyes glowing blue, "You and your kind belong in the Dream. Who gave you leave to own this human?" With his full attention fixed on the Taken, Tom was doing his own set of calculations. Nightmares were dark beings that lived within the Dream. They rarely bothered themselves with the People, but for reasons Tom didn't know, were actively hostile to humans. And, he was somehow certain, they would be particularly hostile to the Bright One. They were always about some great task or mission, which meant this one was not here by accident. Whatever its purpose here, Tom would never be able to convince the human Telestry to help him with this entity in the way.

The Taken laughed again, "This one gave me *everything* long ago. He has become a part of myself. He wouldn't even live without me, now."

The Telestics shifted uneasily as Tom stared at the being, poised on a razor's edge. Whatever this human had once been, he had given himself over to the Nightmare completely. If Tom could kill the human vessel, the Nightmare would rebound into the Dream. It might find him again, someday, and this was SO much more powerful than the one he'd angered in Bounty City that he could hardly believe what he was contemplating. Still, IF he could kill the puppet...

Again, the Nightmare calculated his intent correctly. This time, its laugh was malevolent. "Try me, *pup*."

Tom very nearly did.

He was saved from his decision, at least momentarily, by a shout from behind him.

Tom risked one glance backward to see a group of short figures in simple, white gi running toward them. Almost instantly, he refocused his gaze on the Taken, who he was satisfied to see looked genuinely shocked. Anything that could shock an Archon could also give Tom an advantage, and he needed one desperately. Tom fixed his gaze on the Taken, which was now splitting its attention between Tom and the group of humans he could hear running up behind him.

They might attack, but probably not. He sensed something familiar, and his instincts were saying they wouldn't hurt him. He had no choice but to trust those instincts. The Taken was more than dangerous enough all on its own. Tom began edging toward the wall on his left, not wanting to be between these newcomers and the Telestics. He had come seeking the Bright One—now all he wanted was to extract himself from the situation, preferably with his matrix intact.

When Tom was close enough to the wall that he could see both the Taken and the human pups at the same time, he stopped and simply watched.

The Taken's host hadn't moved, but within the dream, its form stilled, like a predator waiting to pounce. It watched the approaching humans with an emotion Tom couldn't parse. Not fear, he thought. Uncertainty, perhaps?

Tom turned more of his attention on the newcomers. He had trouble telling humans apart, even now, but was that...?

One of the humans preempted his thought. A female with long, brown hair frowned at Tom for a moment, then pointed right at him, "He's the one from Bounty City, Andrew." She nodded warily in Tom's direction and he returned her nod of acknowledgment with one of his own. The boy at the head of the group glanced over at him quickly, nodding as well, "OK, Rachel." Then he returned his gaze to the Telestics before them.

The little group of human youths stopped in front of the Telestics, while Tom stood to one side, his eyes still fixed on the Taken. Even with his attention on that immeasurably dangerous being, Tom could feel the anger and determination radiating from the youths' leader, Andrew. The rest of the little group was split between determined and disheartened. One or two looked ready to positively tear down the spires around them. Others trailed behind their leader with heads downcast, hardly seeing their surroundings at all.

It was a strange contrast, but before Tom could divine its cause, the human Telestic who had first addressed Tom stepped forward once more to meet this new group, already raising a hand for them to stop—totally unnecessarily it seemed to Tom. "Who are you, and what business do you have in the Telestry?"

The one called Andrew pointed up to the tiny, sparkling red dot above them and snapped back, "Brightstar's been captured. It's your fault. You have to fix this." He visibly swallowed and moderated his tone. "We can't handle them. We need help...please?"

The woman shook her head sharply, even as his plea hung in the air, "The Telestry cannot afford to insert itsel..."

The Taken cut her off, contempt leaching from every pore of the host while in the Dream its substance roiled with its words, "The Telestry is *OUR* creature. It was Drake Loriden, the chief priest himself, who *ASKED* the Dominion to take custody of your precious Brightstar! Even now, he is..." The Taken himself was cut off mid-sentence in a blur of motion.

At first, Tom wasn't sure what exactly had happened. ... Had he blinked? No... The girl with the brown hair—Rachel—stood where the Taken had been, her eyes flashing. As Tom watched, she massaged her fist, looking satisfied. Had she *punched* the Taken?? How had she moved so fast? Not even The People could move that fast.

Despite the shocked silence, her mutter was so quiet that a human would never have heard her, as Tom did, "You don't talk about Brightstar."

Tom's gaze flickered down the lane behind the Telestics, searching, and his eyes widened. Whatever Rachel did had launched it more than fifty feet down the lane, and where it landed the pavement was crumpled into ruin. As Tom watched, the being lifted itself clumsily out of the shattered depression its landing had created, one arm dangling strangely.

Then it let out an unearthly howl.

"*I am the REAPER of SOULLLLLLLSSSSSSS!*"

The substance of the Dream vibrated with the Archon's anger, the dissonance between the Dream and the physical clawing at Tom's brain.

Rachel stared at the Taken dumbfounded while Tom was left in shock as powerful as that which had taken him in Bounty City. She had *punched* the Taken of an Archon! How could she do such a thing? How could she have the *power* to do such a thing without even knowing what she was doing?! Could even one so powerful as she not even SEE an Archon?

The Taken was actually levitating into the air in its fury as it pointed one bone-white finger at Rachel.

"*I am the maker of MATRIIIIXXXXXX.*"

Tom's own matrix quivered, forcing him to grit his teeth against the vibration of the dream as the Archon howled.

The Archon began to suck in power from both the dream and the world around like a black hole drawing in every bit of light it could reach. The brilliance formed a dawn-like halo around the Nightmare, and the Archon's shadowy shape finally came clear. The Archon looked...like Tom. With something between horror and awe dawning within him, Tom realized who and what this creature must be. It was The Reaper, progenitor of The People—perhaps not all of The People, but of Tom's own people certainly.

In all the legends of The People, there was no Archon more powerful than The Reaper. None could challenge it outright, and even the Lightmaker Himself had once given it a place of honor—long, long before...

The Taken, of course, hadn't paused to give respect to Tom's epiphany.

"*A HUMAN has the temerity to attack MEEEEEE...*"

Its head was thrown back, and Tom could tell a tremendous wave of power was gathering within the Archon's core. It was like tasting ozone in the air before electricity jumped, fulfilling its potential. But, once again,

Reaper's word was chopped off as if with a knife.

Focused as he was, Tom saw the streak as Rachel's dark hair streamed behind her in her near teleportation forward. With its head thrown back, Reaper had missed it, and the crack of her fist hitting it directly in the jaw was shockingly loud.

This time, though, Reaper didn't just collapse. It was still thrown backward as before, but the energy that had gathered within it exploded. The power ripped outward, throwing Rachel backward as well and knocking several of the Telestics completely off their feet. One of the weaker Telestic's shields flickered out, and the buildings around them tremored like a bell struck by a colossal hammer.

Tom cowered. Just looking at the Archon he could see that the human anchoring it to this world still wasn't dead, though Rachel's blow should have crushed any mortal's skull to powder. Indeed, as Tom watched from the shadow of the wall, shell shocked and bewildered, it rose once more. The girl must have broken its jaw, because this time Reaper gargled instead of speaking.

*"*ARRGHGAAAARRRRHHGGAAA!!!*"*

The fact that its words in the Dream were hardly more coherent than what its meat puppet uttered didn't even tempt Tom to laugh, the specter of its wrath was so terrifying. Raw power roared out from the being like a gale-force wind, and a few of the Telestics must have either failed to shield themselves or, as was obviously true of one man, had their shields ripped away by the initial blast, because the power that streamed across them began to strip flesh from their bones as Tom watched. He felt the strain on his own shield, still tolerable but increasing as the seconds passed.

The youths in white were completely unaffected. Even Rachel had managed to maintain her shield when the blast hit her, though it had knocked her flying.

Tom saw Andrew step forward with a quiet epithet, as he saw what the radiating power was doing to the Telestics. The human boy extended his own shield to cover them—too late for the two who had been unshielded, but fortunately for two of the others, who immediately collapsed. Tom could tell the human boy was still hardly exerting himself, only looking annoyed.

The buildings around them, on the other hand, were taking a beating as cracks formed in their surfaces and the underlying energy that held them aloft was flayed away to be sucked into Reaper's matrix. Tom could see telltale energy patterns disappearing into the crystalline flesh the Archon had somehow grown inside its human host. Tom winced at the sheer volume of Energy streaming from Reaper to rip the power from its surroundings and return it, in a great howling arc, to its center. How much Energy must it carry within its matrix for this to be possible? Even as he watched, Reaper reached out toward the girl who had struck it, now sprawled on the ground several paces away, and clenched its fist, obviously attempting to draw her life Energy from her by main force.

It might have worked if the other youths hadn't stepped forward and... joined their shields to hers? Was that possible? Tom shook his head, bewildered once more, as Reaper's attempt to drain her succeeded only in glutting even the Archon's insatiable matrix. The Archon drew in enough energy in the space of an eye blink that if Tom were in its place, his own matrix would have overloaded in a catastrophic explosion.

Andrew's lips tightened and he shook his head. "I don't know what you are, but if you know anything of what has happened to Brightstar..."

"*ARROOOOOOOOOOAAAAAWWWW!!!*"

Once more, the sheer substance and volume of Reaper's howl cut him off and its assault renewed, this time battering at the little group's shield like the impact of a kinetic energy weapon striking them from orbit. The walls around them splintered and crumbled, their masonry and alloy crumpling back from the blow as Reaper tried to crush the insignificant human specks that had *dared* defy it.

Tom still cowered by the wall, unspeakably grateful that he had been interrupted before he could attempt to destroy Reaper's human anchor. He wouldn't be able to withstand even a fraction of that power.

The human youths barely seemed phased, though the ones that had been downcast or self-absorbed had perked up. Tom caught Andrew glancing at him, giving him a half-smirk, expanding his own shield once again to cover Tom, barely in time.

Reaper's next attack was unspeakable in its violence. It was as if darkness incarnate reached out of the ground, forming into a tremendous fist to hammer them into oblivion.

In the midst of the shield, two of the older boys looked at each other and nodded, then stepped forward. Their own riposte to Reaper's attack was just as powerful, stabbing out of their shield to pierce the Archon with the primordial Energy of the universe.

It had no effect. Whether Reaper absorbed the blow or simply phased past it, Tom couldn't tell. In that moment, however, he knew what had to be done. Reaper's anchor must be destroyed, even at the cost of the entire Telestry around them.

"Destroy his vessel!" Tom called from lungs that felt raw and flayed. Then, he shut himself away from both the dream and the world around him, searching his core for the strength to do what he knew he must. Around him, the battle continued, with the youths doing everything possible to defeat the immortal Archon. Tom ignored it.

He fell to his hands and knees, reaching down into the dirt toward the threads of power that secured the very ground on which they stood. He had sensed those threads what felt like a week ago, when he stood before the Telestry gate. All he had to do was to break enough of them... Tom consumed the Energy that held the earth stable, trying to break the bonds and release the pent-up volcanic wrath. He was succeeding. He was almost there. Then, distantly, he heard a bellow like a wounded bull and something crushed his perceptions.

It was like getting caught with his hand in an amphora. Reaper had seen his attempt to destroy the stability of the land beneath the Telestry and now, like fingers extended into a metaphorical jar, Tom's being had poked out from under the shield Andrew extended around him. Reaper caught his mental hand and tried to crush him, eliciting pain the likes of which Tom had only felt once before. Then, the Archon pulled.

It was as if the hand of a god was trying to remove his spirit from his body by brute force—no, that's exactly what was happening. Tom cursed himself for his blindness. Reaper was the source of The Peoples' ability to siphon Energy from humans, but in the Archon it wasn't just an ability to gather Energy. He was ripping away the essence of Tom's very soul.

Tom had been near to death more than once, but this was unlike anything he'd experienced before. He felt like he was simultaneously being pulled through a tiny hole and his self was ripping out of his body. It was both unbearable and inescapable, and it seemed to last an eternity.

When the end finally came, with a mind-jarring snap, at first Tom was certain he must be dead. Instead, Tom found he could still see, though his mind felt warped and twisted and he wasn't really sure what he was seeing. A tall Telestic—tall for a human—stood above...something on the ground. She stared down at whatever it was with something between contempt and fury, looking around at the destruction that surrounded them—it was the Telestic woman who had first spoken to Tom.

There was a molten glow off to one side. Tom could only guess he had partially succeeded in his aim to bring the planet's core to the surface. More obviously, the bases of the towers immediately around them were reduced to ruined shards. Their tops somehow, impossibly, hung by the bridges that connected them to their neighbors. The destruction was as surreal as the Telestry's beauty still surrounding it.

After a moment, the Telestic said, "Stratograve Rectis was always a slime mold. He should have died a hundred years ago. I guess now we know why he didn't." Tom would have sworn she spat on...was that the corpse of Reaper's anchor?

Andrew laughed grimly, "So, I hope that at least changes your answer. We need your help, Telestic."

The woman sniffed, "My name is Melindra Malleus, and you have no idea what you're asking. The Brightstar has been taken to Polestar station, the seat of the Dominion. The Telestry's hands are tied."

Rachel laughed grimly, derisively, "We'd hate to inconvenience you. It's only the Brightstar's life we're talking about. You're right that you don't have a choice... But you're wrong about the way this has to end."

The woman was still completely unphased, her tone iron-hard, "Even I don't have the power to move the Telestry to the Brightstar's aid. Only Drake Loriden could make that decision, and he's already made another."

Another of the human youths, a girl, started to interrupt, but Malleus raised her hand commandingly and drove over the interruption, "Unfortunately, the council agrees with our Chief Councilor. Without their support, I can do nothing except leave the Telestry myself."

Andrew's reply was obviously desperate, "Then you can help us? Even if the Telestry won't?"

Malleus's laugh was hammered steel, "Alone, my strength is far less than even one of you, child. What do you want from me? Our deceased friend Rectis wasn't wrong. The Telestry is Their creature. I should have left long ago, before..."

Without finishing the sentence, she turned to go, the other Telestics trailing behind her. She paused only to call back to them, "You should find your own way out, Odds. As of this moment, I have no power to extend you hospitality."

The extraordinary group of youths for whom power seemed no object stared after the retreating Telestic for a long time while Tom regathered himself.

When he was able to stand again, he looked around once, then turned his gaze to the heavens from whose depths he had come in hopes of finding a savior. There, in the sky above, pulsed the red bead of light that Tom now knew was called Polestar.

Tom's close encounter with the Reaper now gave him a new insight into the source of the red haze that seemed to engulf Polestar. It was the presence of unimaginable power and darkness, concentrated so heavily that it leached out, staining the Dream red. Whatever force was present there, it must be a thousand times stronger than the Reaper—a million times stronger.

He stared out at the glowing speck for a long time without speaking, then threw back his head and let out a howl so loud and keening that a few of the humans clapped their hands over their ears.

His grief and despair offered to the night, Tom stood still again, simply staring at the ugly speck of brilliance.

"It is too late, then," he said softly. "The bright one has gone to the seat of the starkillers."

Finally, he turned his head and looked down, giving each of the youths in turn a long look.

No one answered.

Tom bowed his head, deep pain and sorrow blossoming once more in his core, "Then we are lost."

In the blackness above, Polestar station looked like nothing so much as the red eye of a far-off dragon, glaring unblinkingly down at them through the void.

Tom Nelion's strange odyssey concluded in alliance with the 'Odds' who followed the Brightstar. It began with the death of those he loved most, in the most ignominious circumstances any of The People could possibly imagine.

Author's Note: I've been told this story is difficult for some readers to immerse themselves in. The reason seems obvious to me —living in an alien being's thoughts is not for everyone. (I really did try to create a sense of what it must be to live as one of The People for this story.) If that doesn't appeal to you, dear reader, I offer my apologies. My hope, however, is to leave you with a window into the world of Tom Nelion, the inimitable Boy From The Darkness.

Nosuferian Outcast, Ep 1:
The Boy from the Megalith

Year 2220 NST – The Void, Aurora Galaxy

Tom Nelion cowered against the deck, hatred filling his soul. "Now, I'ma drain you too, whelp." Bausgh's ugly, puggish face was twisted into an even uglier expression as he stepped forward, sneering down at Tom through bloodshot eyes.

Tom bent his head, fighting shock and trying not to stare at the gray corpses of his clan, now slowly crumbling to dust behind the shining bulk of the brute that towered over him. Baush was almost too bright to look at, and he must have seen the pain in Tom's eyes when he tried to look up then had to turn his head away.

Baush laughed, his contempt crushing Tom to the deck even harder than the wave of blue Energy that Baush ground mercilessly into him. It was all Tom could do to keep breathing. Around him stood a half circle of Baush's clan mates and three other alphas. At least they weren't smirking. Two looked worried. The others were simply solemn.

"Your chief shouldn'a challenged me. Now you *all* get'ta see why Baush is Boss." He laughed again, obviously pleased with his wordplay.

The fact that Baush was so wrong—and so abyssally stupid—was doubly hard to take. Tom's chief—his father, Nelion—had only been trying to make a point to the other alpha. Now he was dead, and Tom was about to be.

The first lance of pain took Tom's breath away completely as Baush reached into Tom's Ka and began ripping away the Energy of life. Agony writhed up and down his nerves, radiating from his core, where his Ka lived, out into his limbs. His body was consuming itself, and the torture had just begun. Tom was lost in the pain even before he felt the top layer of his aura siphoned away and Baush began feeding in earnest.

Tom's clan had not forgotten him, though, even in death. The moment lasted an eternity, then an ancestral Ikhu came upon Tom and the pain faded into white-hot rage. He was still trapped, could still feel his life Energy being drawn into the crystalline matrices of Baush's body, but his need for relief was replaced with an unquenchable desire to destroy the monster who had already killed his clan.

Tom struggled in vain, howling as he felt the fabric of his very soul being ripped away from him, desperate to get at Baush.

It was futile.

Then, without warning, the torment stopped. Baush laughed again as Tom's body equalized, the Energy in his matrix re-stabilizing and refilling the hole Baush had made in his core. It left Tom's entire being weaker. Tom gasped, his rage forgotten in the relief, but it was short lived.

"I'm'a make you cry, tiny. Your chief should'a spaced you when you were whelped. Man-spawn."

Then the pain was back and somehow, impossibly, it was even worse than before. Tom wasn't sure how long it lasted. It could have been a minute or a day. Four more agonizing, unbearable times, Baush stopped short of actually killing Tom to taunt him and allow his life Energy to seep from his body, refilling his core less and less completely each time. At some point, Tom lost himself in the Ikhu, which crowded around him, many trying to comfort him as his essence was slowly depleted.

At some point, full awareness returned—Tom wasn't sure why. He could feel death's chilly breath on his face and his eyelids fluttered. Baush had stopped. It had been too long. Why wasn't he dead? An unconscious whine escaped his lips. From above, he heard Baush grunt. As if from a great distance a voice said, "...wish this one for myself." Dimly, he recognized Ilya, Baush's alpha female.

Baush snarled. "The lesson must be. I am King Chief."

Ilya's derision wasn't hidden, but compared to the bludgeon of Baush's dull wit, she was a scalpel—precise and cutting. "If you kill every chief who is lesser, then what will you be? King of the floating dustbin?"

Baush grumbled something incoherent, and Tom strained to raise his head, trying to see.

Ilya's eyes glittered. She mocked, "Baush so big-strong, Baush kill all tribe 'til Baush alone."

Baush took a step toward Ilya as if to strike her, but she pointed to her belly and her mocking deepened. "Baush so big-strong! Crush pregnant she!"

Baush's grumbling turned into a roar. He threw his hands up in the air and turned to stomp away. Almost instantly, the little gaggle of whipped underlings began to disperse, only pausing to bow to Ilya, completely ignoring Tom's crumpled body.

Tom tried to move and failed. His head dropped back onto the floor, and he heard Ilya's breathing as she stepped closer. Tom squeezed his eyes shut, waiting for her to finish what Baush had started, but instead she hissed.

All he caught of her mutter was a single, phrase, half-slurred, "the remnant..." The next thing Tom knew, he was being lifted off the deck. Tom could still feel death's cold fingers, stroking his chest where his Ka flickered and guttered inside him. Its pull was inevitable, inexorable. He succumbed slowly, not wanting to die but too weak to resist.

Tom must have passed out again, because when he awoke, he was falling. In one frozen instant, Tom saw Ilya, her disgust plain on her face, framed by the walls of the feeding pit that stretched almost out of sight above him. Then he hit bottom. It didn't really hurt. The People were built tough, but he was still practically unable to move because of how thoroughly Baush had drained him. He lay there for a long moment, feeling the pull of death. It would be a sweet relief from his current state. Then he saw the humans. The Ikhu must have been hovering near, because in an instant he was consumed with hunger and his vision went blood red.

What happened next was a semi-conscious blur. The Ikhu had full control of his body, and his Ka was so weak he couldn't have stopped even if he wanted to. All Tom felt was hunger. Physical pain registered dimly as he ran into... something, but his vision was completely black. There was a sound, far away. Without warning, a sweet, powerful sensation carried his consciousness away completely. It had a sharp, pungent feeling that made him distantly uncomfortable, but he was too caught up in the moment to care. When the Ikhu released control of Tom's senses and his volition returned, he was standing over a spreading pile of dust, with Ilya cursing him from above.

"Void-brained fool whelp! She was *breeding stock!*" Ilya seemed on the verge of jumping down just to punish him, but when she saw him looking up, his eyes clear once more, she simply turned and walked away, snarling to herself. The heavy alloy door slid down from above, trapping Tom in the feeding pit with the humans. If he'd been at full strength, he would have simply leapt out of the pit and rolled under the door, but in his current state that was laughable. All he could do was watch it close.

This was the lowest moment of Tom's life. The feeding pit's impossibly high walls towered over him, their micrometrically-precise lines impassive to his desolation. Before, he had been too busy for the sheer magnitude of his loss to hit home. The confrontation with Baush had been too intense, death too near. Now, with the burst of energy he'd gained from draining the human she, the vision still burned into his eyes of the alpha queen's retreating back, he felt as if the Monolith had been pulled from under him, leaving him floating in the empty blackness of the void. Clanless, alone and empty, just like the void surrounding the Monolith.

Tom laid back his head and keened his loss to the uncaring stars.

When he looked back down, one of the humans was scuttling away from him, something clutched in its five-fingered hand. The little man stared absolute hatred at

Tom, his face a rictus. Then the human sighed and slid down the wall to sit with head in his hands, staring at the remnant of the human that Tom had just turned into a dust pile.

Tom felt a stab of shame at Ilya's displeasure. He hadn't meant to do it. It had been the Ikhu, the ancestor spirit. The People were reduced, somehow, when they died. It was as if the living being was distilled to the essence of their personality, a mere shadow of a living being. The People didn't leave navettas like humans. Instead, their spirits were released to roam the universe. Inevitably, the thought called Tom's mother to his mind and he wondered what had happened to her navetta. With Nelion dead, Tom would probably never know.

The human, now huddled against the wall across from Tom, was still staring, tears running down his cheeks. Tom turned his face away and, sighing, concentrated on leeching what Energy he could from the little group of humans without actually killing them.

Humans were strange. They consumed actual matter as sustenance and the Energy gathered around them purely because they were alive. Some could use the Energy on purpose, while others were just dumb animals. The People were something different. They existed in a place half-way between the universe and somewhere else. The Energy didn't hurt Tom when he used it as it did humans, but the only way he could replenish his reserves was by pulling it from the world around him, especially from humans. None of the People had ever been quite sure why the Energy was so strong around humans, but it was, and so they became the People's primary source of food.

A few among them groaned or whimpered, but none tried to attack him. They had learned long ago that the cost of attacking one of the People was death.

The siphon was slow. At the fastest rate he could manage, he wouldn't be back to full strength for days, even after having accidentally killed the first human, taking her Energy in a burst. Guilt pricked at Tom now that he'd had time to settle down and think about the she's death, but it was over now. Even the People couldn't turn back time.

Tom was tired. His burst of energy was finally wearing off, and the room blurred around him.

He lay down, keeping his siphon open and fading slowly, inexorably into the Fugue.

Tom's Dream was dark, though he could still vaguely sense the world around him. The flow of time stretched into something variable and strange. The humans went about their meager business, eating and sleeping but keeping as far from Tom as they could while Tom's consciousness was taken by the Dream.

Around him, the Ikhu of his clan swarmed. They were like the roaches that sometimes spawned in the humans' food supply. Beyond, the greater denizens of the Dream lurked. They preyed upon the minds of the humans while they slept, but most were afraid of the People.

Visions came and went, obscuring the Dream with flashes of past and present as well as possible futures still unrealized. The visions were all dark, flavored by a hopelessness that seeped into his bones. It hadn't always been so. Tom could remember a time when the visions had been different, but now? The universe was being consumed by evil, though he could only see it clearly within the Dream.

It was only because of the darkness that Tom could see the light when it appeared. It was so far away that at first he thought he'd imagined it. However faint, it didn't flicker or fade. It was a single light, far away, shining like a beacon in the darkness and deeper darkness of the Dream.

Even as his concentration was interrupted by a particularly vivid memory of his mother, Tom wondered at that tiny point of light.

Time passed strangely in the Fugue, but Tom could dimly sense the siphon, still slowly regenerating the Energy of his matrix, sometimes fast and sometimes slow. His subjective sense of time ebbed and flowed. Dreams and visions came and went, their tendrils passing him from one to the next for what might have been hours, days or weeks. Outside, time might be passing with metronome precision, but here it followed its own rules.

Waking was instantaneous and jarring. He had been dreaming about...what was it? But something was wrong—dreadfully wrong.

Tom looked around. Nothing seemed amiss at first glance. Most of the humans were asleep. Even the Energy gave him no hint as to what might be happening, and there was no noise beyond the sounds of Megalith, the ship that had been his home his whole life. The sounds were comforting, likely the single most constant factor in his existence. The only time he could remember the sounds changing was when the great vessel had been shut down for maintenance when he was a child, before Baush had become king chief.

Tom could hardly remember it. He had been barely more than a pup at the time.

Then he heard it again. There had been a scraping sound, as of metal on metal. The sound came from outside the single door above him. Tom frowned in puzzlement and opened his inner eye beyond its usual slit. There *was* something beyond that door. He wasn't certain what it was, but it had the strangest Energy pattern Tom had ever seen. It was all disjointed angles and impossibly thin lines. How were such strange angles even possible with the Energy of life? It clung to the body, and that wasn't the shape of any body he recognized...

Then, a talon...or was it an arm? slashed down *through* the alloy of the door. One of the humans screamed and Tom was on his feet, Energy gathering in his palms.

Another strike followed, then another, each tearing the ragged hole wider. Tom bared his teeth.

A Bug.

What was *that* doing in Megalith? Two more blows screamed down to further rend the metal and Tom allowed the Energy to fade from his hands, a primal rage suffusing him. This was the first Bug that had ever breached Megalith... It must be made to pay. Simply bathing it in the cleansing fire of the Energy was not enough to purge such a dishonor to the People.

Tom crouched, then leapt the twelve feet straight up to the door just as the monster slashed again. Tom reached through the gaping hole the monster had torn to grasp its retreating talon, wrenching the appendage back through the hole.

The thing made a strangled, surprised screeching sound as Tom braced his feet against the door on either side of the great gash, still holding fast to its arm. Using the monster as an anchor, he held himself in place and reached his other hand through the gap, trying to grasp anything within range. His fingers slipped off the thing's slick, hard exoskeleton and he growled deep in his throat, then reached up higher on the arm he held and began pulling the creature toward the ragged hole. As if he were climbing hand-over-hand up a rope, he drew the monster's limb through the hole.

It screeched again, this time in panic as Tom hauled on that arm with the implacable strength of the People. Then, he could see the juncture where the limb met its body and he twisted, feeling the limb crack as he shoved it upward at an unnatural angle. He reached through the hole again, his hand scrabbling once more off the monster's carapace. After a furious, desperate moment, he found purchase, catching the edge of one of its armored plates and heaving.

The monster thrashed madly now as he drew it inexorably toward him, finally releasing the broken limb to reach through the hole and catch hold of another of the beast's plates. Then, Tom had a real hold on its body, and he howled his triumph. His vision went red as the Ikhu took him once more.

The next few seconds passed in a blur. Tom's vision was completely black and he felt as if the strength of a thousand of the People coursed through him.

What had been an inexorable pull became a tremendous heave, and he wrenched the Bug's body through the hole it had made in the alloy of the door. It was like putting a moth through a fan. Carapace crumpled and gore exploded across Tom's body. He howled again, his vision slowly clearing as the life fled from the creature's broken husk, shredded by its passage through a hole far too small for it.

His effort had unbalanced him and he fell, the twitching wreckage of what had, a moment ago, been a living Bug still clutched in his hands.

Tom released the creature's corpse in mid-air and twisted to bring his feet back under him. He snarled to himself, belatedly realizing that he *should* have tried to drain the monster instead of simply shredding it. The Ikhu were troublesome, and letting them become the master, even for a moment, was stupid and dangerous.

Tom landed in a crouch, then threw his head back and howled. However wasteful he'd been, his triumph was sweet, and he savored it...until he looked up to see another of the creatures climbing through the hole in the door above. Wrenching the first Bug through the hole had widened it just enough for the next to wriggle through intact, and there was another behind it.

He barely had time to set himself before the first one jumped—straight at him. Tom lost sight of the second monster as he pivoted to avoid the leap, and the creature landed directly in front of him. Tom bared his fangs and leapt forward, grasping for it. No Bug would invade his home while he lived.

This time, his struggle was blur in his conscious mind, his opponent a mass of thrashing limbs and mandibles. He registered very little except the monster's beady, black eyes and his own rage, partly because he had to expend almost as much energy fighting off the Ikhu as the Bug. He would not lose control again—and he didn't, not this time. Twice, he tried draining the Bug, but its hide was resistant to the Energy. It shrugged off his attempts, breaking his concentration both times by slashing at him.

After what felt like an hour of dodging and maneuvering, Tom finally managed to get beside the monster. It was all he needed. With a snarl, he seized the joint where one leg met its body and pulled. Bugs were dangerous, but the People were stronger. The crystalline matrix of Tom's body flowed with the Energy of Life, and he wrenched at the leg–ineffectually. His body was still starved of Energy. He felt weak, almost feeble despite his rage, twisting the creature's leg. It squealed and screeched, then started thrashing.

Tom gritted his teeth and redoubled his efforts, wrenching hard. There was a pop and the leg actually pulled out of the Bug's abdomen. Tom smiled darkly and stuck his hand inside the hole, now pumping ichor. Sweet Energy flowed into his matrix, directly out of the thing's body. It was helpless before him without its hide to shield against the Energy.

The Bug went mad, thrashing at him in a frenzy of sharp limbs and something that looked like spiky, prehensile wings, but only for a moment. Its body puffed to dust as Tom laid back his head and howled, the monster's very life suffusing him, becoming his own.

His triumph only lasted a moment. He stared around, trying to find the other. Where had it gone?

Ahh. He spotted it in the corner across from him, crouched over something, and reached out with his newly acquired Energy, grabbing the Bug from behind with ropes of green power and dragging it toward him. It turned as he pulled and sprang straight at him, and this one was so close he couldn't dodge.

The Bug crashed into Tom's chest, scrabbling at him with its mandibles as one scythe-like appendage slashed down toward his head. Tom kicked the thing in the head to push that maw away from him, as all four of its insectoid arms windmilled, trying to slash him. Through his rage, a note of caution reached him from his more sensible side. The monster's huge talons could open him up like a rotten sack, with or without his crystalline skin.

One arm darted toward him, searching for an opening. He caught the descending blow in an open palm, twisted the creature's appendage around, and strained until it snapped with a satisfying *crackk*. He was stronger now. Much stronger. He gloried in his power as the creature flailed, keening.

The only problem was, it still had three arms, all reaching for him at once, and he was in front of this one rather than beside it. Tom dodged and blocked, using the Energy to entangle one appendage while the other two slashed at the wall beside him.

The Bug pressed him backward into the corner, its mandibles extending, and Tom tripped, falling flat on his back as it crawled over him. Tom straight-armed the thing in its hideous face, trying to push it back, but only found his hand inside the foul creature's writhing maw, its mandibles slicing impossibly through the crystalline skin of his arm.

Tom smiled and clamped down with his fingers, grasping the inside of its throat and reaching out to rip the Energy of Life out of its body.

This one didn't thrash. Instead, its body seized and twitched, then crumbled to icy cold dust, covering him in the foul-smelling stuff. The dissonance between the almost unbearably sweet flow of power into his core as the monster crumbled and the unpleasant sensation of being covered in its remains was distantly repugnant, but then Tom was lost to the world. For a long, sweet moment, he reveled in the hot euphoria as the skin of his forearm knit back together where the monster had slashed him.

As some measure of reality returned, Tom blinked, trying to clear his eyes. There could be more of them. He fought to regain his bearings.

Then he froze.

The razor-sharp tip of a talon hovered directly between his eyes, wobbling slightly.

It took a moment for his vision to trace the talon up the creature's arm, and it took another moment for his confusion to clear. The human male was there, the severed arm clutched in his hands, blood flowing from a gash on his face, more slicking his side as he gasped, hatred shining from his eyes.

The man's bloody visage glaring at him as the talon before his face wobbled more and more. The man had been fighting the second Bug, using this torn-off limb from the first that Tom had wrenched through the door. Tom remembered the final Bug crouched over the human, and Tom could see from the blood pumping from the man's side that it had hurt him badly. It must have been on the very edge of finishing him when Tom pulled it off.

Tom stared into those eyes as the talon scraped his forehead, its impossibly-sharp blade scoring his crystalline skin. He had killed the man's mate, and now the man himself was dying where he stood, his life blood pumping out on Megalith's deck.

It was a single moment, frozen in time, upon which Tom's life and that of the human hung. The borrowed weapon was practically touching Tom's eye. Perhaps he could have moved, could have snatched it away, but the anguish written on that human face moved him in a way he hadn't felt since before his mother... Then the severed limb clattered to the floor and the man turned away, his face a mask of pain that plainly came as much from his heart as from his wounds, grievous as they were.

Tom stared after him. Then, with a sigh that turned into a snort as dust half choked him, he staggered to his feet to follow the retreating human.

Two steps later, the man collapsed and Tom was there to catch him, his own body now fortified by the Energy the bugs had so unwillingly provided him. Tom was no healer, but the human was going to die if he didn't act.

He reached out with the Energy of life, using the death he had inflicted on his enemies—and that which he had taken from the man's own mate—to restore life to one who justly hated him.

About the Author

Jared N. Michaud is a devoted fiction writer driven by a passion for writing that began before he reached age seven. Influenced by literary giants like C.S. Lewis and Orson Scott Card, he discovered the power of storytelling, and at twelve he began crafting his first novel.

© 2023 - Rachel Collins Photography LLC

Today, Jared writes from a little house in a little town in Wyoming, where he lives with his wife and six children. As a Christian with a deep love for the truth and appreciation for the values that underlie Western civilization, he endeavors to create myths that will inspire future generations.

The Vale of Mysteries

The Epimyth - Book 2

When they had all donned suits, they crowded out the airlock to make the short hop over to Hope One. A spacewalk outside was somehow a much different experience than being inside the Behemoth. The infinitude of space had a weight that drove itself instantly into the consciousness, even inside the Vale with the tremendous dust clouds surrounding them on every side, refracting rainbows from the incredible power of Sanctuary's blue-white sun. They all felt it, as attested by the silence over their suit radios once Adamant's airlock had opened. Each of them pushed off gently from Adamant toward the airlock on Hope One, which they could already see had handholds surrounding it. They reached it one by one and they all managed to grab on without trouble.

By mutual unspoken agreement, they allowed Rachel to examine the airlock's controls. After a brief once over, she announced, "It's coded."

There was a moment of silence, then Jon said, "Try Trisha."

"Oh," Rachel said, but she keyed something in and a moment later the light on the airlock glowed and it slid open, silent in the vacuum. "That was mom's name," she said after a moment. "Dad must have expected it would be us. I mean I know Teron said he had, but..." She trailed off and pulled herself forward into the airlock.

Considering the size of the ship, the airlock was surprisingly small, barely big enough for five of them at once. As it cycled, Shannon remarked, "It's amazing that this stuff still works. It's been a thousand years, right? And that's like three thousand earth years." She looked a bit overwhelmed by the sheer amount of time.

Rachel shook her head, half smiling in memory. "Dad always had a knack for leaving things so they'd work when they were needed. It was one of his talents. Besides, null gravity makes a lot of difference, and it's all been asleep."

A moment later, Laura commented, "I think there's even air in here. Not sure whether it's breathable."

A quick look into the fields confirmed that she was right, and as the airlock opened into the ship itself, Nate unsealed his helmet. The air inside Hope One smelled like machinery and old grease, but Nate didn't have any trouble breathing it, and light flooded into the airlock from the corridor beyond.

After a moment, Jon noticed what Nate had done and he frowned. "You know that could have killed you, right?"

Nate grinned crookedly and popped his helmet loose completely. After a little consideration the others followed his example and Nate said thoughtfully, "The others should be through soon enough. I'm not sure about you guys, but since the air's good I'm going to leave my suit here."

After a moment, nods went around the group and all five of them proceeded to strip their suits off. Once the airlock had cycled open again and the rest of the group was busy stripping off their own suits, Rachel turned down the passage to her right and began pulling herself along via handholds recessed into the wall. Jon, Nate and Shannon followed silently, with Jon behind Rachel and Nate bringing up the rear behind Shannon.

The lights in Hope One came on well ahead of them and went off again once they had passed, but even in the space directly around them the corridors of the ship were dimly lit. Some of the lights had failed with time, and a thin layer of fine dust had collected on every surface. Nate had no idea where it might have come from, but they stirred it up as they passed, making him sneeze now and then, following as he was.

The trip from the airlock forward took what felt like an age, and they made it in silence, buried in their own thoughts. Finally, Rachel came to another closed hatch, which she took only a moment to open. The corridor beyond turned at a right angle and Nate realized what they'd been pulling themselves along was actually a ladder way. Hope One had been built vertically with the nose pointing upward. What they were entering now was actually a short corridor that crossed the width of the vessel, with a hatch to either side of them and another pointed toward the nose of the craft when they reached the center of the corridor. Rachel stopped again and spent a longer time with this hatch.

Just when Nate was about to ask what she'd found, Rachel smacked the hatch with one hand and, with a resounding crack, it sprang open.

Rachel looked back at Nate with a wry grin. "Aqueous'

privilege. The lock was frozen and it's our ship." She made a face as she ran a hand over the warped hatch frame.

Nate blinked in surprise. "Aqueous?"

"Didn't you know?" She shrugged. "Aqueous specializes in mental or physical force. I got mostly the physical." Rachel pushed through into the next room, which would actually have been above them, Nate realized, if the ship had been oriented properly in a gravity well. It was unmistakably the bridge, and as he followed the others through, Nate looked curiously around. Unlike aboard Adamant, the control stations here were arranged in a circle, and the room's 'ceiling' was further away than either of the walls, suggesting to him that they must be right in the nose of the craft near where the cone came to a point.

All of that was pushed out of his mind by the curious mass in the center of the room. Dominating the massive bridge was a giant cloud, or so it seemed at first glance. The lights mounted around the perimeter of the room and at the control stations didn't illuminate it perfectly, but even so he could see that the mass was roughly spherical, with tendrils and arms extending almost to the control stations that ringed the bridge.

Nate and the others had all caught hold of something, whether the room's broken hatch, in his case, or the nearest control station, in Jon and Rachel's. Shannon was hovering near the wall, her head cocked, staring at the thing.

"It's the Vale," she said, wonder filling her voice.

"I wondered what Dad did to create it," Jon half grumbled. "Looks like we get to see that at least."

Cautiously, Rachel reached forward from where she clung to the control station and passed her hand through one tendril of the cloud, her eyes glued on her hand. No swirl of dust followed her movement. Was the cloud a projection? A hologram?

"Can't feel it," she said.

Nate opened his senses to the fields and examined the cloud. The most obvious feature was a pulsing—a vibration—that brightened and darkened the cloud almost too rapidly for him to perceive. He watched it, fascinated, as the seconds passed and the cloud shifted slowly, waves flowing across its surface. It was an intuition as much as anything that connected the pulsing and the movement in his brain, but suddenly he could see it clearly. The cloud moved the tiniest bit with each pulse of light. It was the light that was causing it to shift and change.

A sudden suspicion crossed Nate's mind and he pushed off gently from the hatch where he clung toward the cloud. It took a moment for him to reach it, but as he passed into it he heard Shannon and Rachel exclaim in surprise.

Rachel called out, "Voids, Nate. Be *careful*." Then his vision was blocked completely. He could still hear without significant muffling, and he could breathe just fine, but his sight was completely obscured by the brownish cloud and his Energematrice6 sense was flooded with the strobing energy that brought the cloud to life.

His reply to Rachel was a tick late, but he managed to inject some humor into it as he floated through the mass. "Well, if there's anything dangerous in here, I'll definitely be the first to find it, even if I can't actually see anything."

Drifting through the cloud, Nate began to move his arms back and forth, feeling for anything solid in the murk. Just when his brain was telling him he must be almost through the other side of the cloud, Nate found what he was looking for with his chest, crashing into it full-on without warning. It didn't move, and the air rushed out of his lungs. Even in zero gravity, inertia had its way. He flailed instinctively, grabbing for the thing with his arms as he bounced off and managed to wrap them around it, pulling himself in. At such close range, the pulses of light that were obviously coming from the thing he'd wrapped himself around were blinding to his Energematrice6 sense. From this range, he could actually feel the energy flowing out of the object into the cloud as if it were moving through his own body. From there, he could distantly sense connections between the cloud around him and the unimaginable vastness of the Vale itself.

Any detail was lost to him at first glance. The pattern was too complex and the pulses were too intense. It was like being blinded by a strobe light while trying to read fine print. He gasped, sucking air back into his lungs, then refocused on the thing—it felt like a big ball—that he had wrapped himself around. He could see the Energematrice6 flowing through the ball, from the center to the outside then back to center again, as rapidly as the strobing, brilliant pulse of energy went through the cloud that represented the Vale. Obviously, it was the source of that dazzling incandescence, but looking inward Nate could see that the Energematrice6 ran through uncountable tiny channels in the globe of crystal. They stretched inside to outside, outside to inside. The channels were both many and one, a collection of myriad tiny veins that were just that, a collection, and that collection was a switch, or possibly a gate. He took in the totality of the object in the tiny space between flashes, then he was blinded again. Some of the channels were closed; more than half, even, but the rest... Hoping he was right, Nate pushed on the collection of channels with his mind and both the flow and the strobing suddenly stopped.

Nate blinked, staring at Jon and Rachel and Shannon. The cloud was gone. Nate moved his head, the motion causing him to drift, his arms still wrapped around the crystal globe, which was now free of whatever had bound it to the center of the ship.

Everyone was speechless for a moment as Nate began to slowly tumble. Rachel said disbelievingly, "I hope you meant to do that. Something tells me Sanctuary's not gonna be real pleased."

Nate shook his head. "I just made it go passive. I don't think I actually shut the Vale off...not exactly." He paused, then added, "Maybe if we brought it back, and gave it to the council? Or..." He trailed off thoughtfully, then shook his head.

Rachel shrugged, but nodded in acceptance. Meanwhile Shannon had pushed off from the wall, flying toward him. She reached out an arm to him and he grabbed it as she floated past, allowing her to pull him into motion toward the opposite wall, one arm still wrapped around the globe.

When Nate finally managed to catch hold of a control console after pushing off the opposite wall, he took a moment to catch his breath. Then, he unwrapped his arm from around the globe and actually looked at it, allowing it to float in front of him in the dimness of the bridge. Even without his Energematrice6 sense, it was breathtaking. If someone could have made a marble the size of a beach ball, then put a living, moving replica of the Vale inside, that was what he beheld. Through his Energematrice6 sense, it was even more spectacular, if for different reasons. Energy in a thousand shades flowed through a myriad of intricate patterns inside it. Nate imagined if he could see the electrons moving through a computer, this is what it might look like.

They all stared at the object for a long time, spellbound, until Jon finally asked, "So now what?"

Nate looked over at Jon, his mouth twisted into a wry grin. "I think we'll take it with us. It may come in handy."

A moment later, Laura poked her helmet-less head through the hatch. "Ahhh. There you are. The others are right behind me." She eyed the globe in front of Nate, her eyebrows raised. "Looks like you already found something, huh? It's pretty."

Shannon snorted. "Yeah, he found it alright."

Then, Tye and Keevan and Jesse and Shawna were all crowding through the hatch into the bridge and exclaiming over the globe. Tye immediately pushed himself off the doorway toward Nate in an effort to see it more closely that ended with Nate trying to grip the console with his legs while holding the globe in one arm and attempting to catch Tye with the other. Then came Shannon's acerbic account of how Nate had come into possession of it, with more emphasis than Nate was really comfortable with on how he'd had no idea what he was actually getting into. She finished with a grin in his direction that made it clear she was at least mostly teasing him.

There were a few good-natured jibes and Keevan moved to examine the globe himself, eventually asking, "What's our objective here? We don't know how much air's left in this heap. Can't be more than a few hours unless the scrubbers are still running." He looked doubtful.

Rachel huffed, "Heap nothing. She's been sitting here for a thousand years and she's still holding air! What other ship can you say that about?"

Keevan shrugged uncomfortably. "No offense intended. After all the talk I've heard about 'the vessel' my whole life, I was practically expecting something magical. My own fault really."

Nate shook his head wryly. "Let's have a look around and see what's here. Anything Jon and Rachel want to look at they can. It's their ship and their show."

They agreed, and spread out to try the other hatches along the corridor that led to the bridge. The first find came almost immediately, as Rachel stuck her head out of a compartment at the end of the hall, calling for Nate. Of course, everyone had to gather again to see what she'd found. Inside what, according to Jon, used to be the captain's private office, metal loops lined one wall. Each loop had a pendant much like those that graced Jon and Rachel's necks attached to it, having drifted to the wall after such a long time in the null gravity. There were three empty loops at one end of the row, but ten of them were still occupied. The pendants' gems were identical in shape to Jon and Rachel's, but the crystal of each amulet was obviously a different color in the light from the room's ceiling fixtures.

Jesse stared at the row of pendants, his eyes widening. "Paul's Amulets! He made twelve of them before he finally created the Sigil. Dad always said they're the most powerful E6 artifacts in the galaxy." He paused for a second then shrugged. "At least, they're the most powerful ones that Paul left behind. Dad was always a little afraid what Paul might have made and never talked about."

Nate pulled himself to a stop at the desk by one wall and looked at the Amulets thoughtfully as the others crowded into the room behind him and Rachel. Noting the three empty loops and the obvious glow coming from the pendants around his, Rachel's and Jon's necks, Nate said, "One for each of you, I think. I'll carry the rest for now."

Tye was, of course, the first to reach them, and after passing his hand over each of the gems, he picked out a light blue crystal that instantly began to glow when he put it around his neck. Tye's eyes immediately grew large and he looked at Nate. "This is so much power! I'm like five Energematrists now! Fifty!"

Nate snorted. "Lightmaker help us all. Remember what I told you about power, will you?"

Tye nodded, grinning, and pushed off for the door, obviously intent on seeing what else he might find.

The others made a ritual of sorts of picking theirs. Shannon was next, passing her hand over each one, frowning, feeling how each interacted with Energematrice6 and settling on a pink crystal that was dark enough to shade almost red. Each in turn did the same. Shawna took the deep green amulet. Keevan took a gray one that barely glowed, even though it seemed just as potent as the others. Laura took a long time when her turn came, eventually choosing a dark blue gem. When his turn finally came, Jesse hesitated, obviously uncertain. Nate frowned thoughtfully and looked Jesse directly in the eyes. "Jesse Galton, will you follow me? Even if it means leaving Sanctuary and all you've ever known?"

Jesse gulped visibly. "I... Yes. Yes, I will."

Nate nodded. "take one."

Jesse's amulet was dark red, leaving four—soft purple,

yellow, brown and turquoise—unclaimed. Nate finally approached, taking those that remained and slipping them carefully into his pocket.

The next find was less interesting for most of them. Jon called out to Rachel from the room that had been their father's as the head of the colony expedition. When she got there, they both bent over a piece of paper pinned to Paul's desk. Nate glanced into the room, but seeing what they were about, he left them to it.

Meanwhile, Shannon had, characteristically, been checking to see if the vessel was functional and to what degree. Nate found her back on the bridge, shaking her head as she paged through screens on an ancient monitor.

Nate grinned. "Bit dated, huh?"

Shannon glanced up at him and returned his grin. "Oh, sure, but I expected that. I'm just amazed at how close the basic design of this system is to Adamant. It's almost like they were built by the same person." Her lips twisted. "Might have been, I guess. No way to know, really, but yeah. I know how it works."

As if on cue, Tye poked his head through the hatch. "Shannon thinks she knows everything." He grinned cheekily at her. "And she's almost right."

Shannon snorted, but she laughed despite herself as Tye pulled his head back out into the passage.

Nate smiled at her and she nodded wryly as if Tye had made a point. "I really don't mean to be a know-it-all."

Nate nodded back, then raised his eyebrows. "So, where do we stand?"

Shannon shook her head. "I wouldn't want to try to move Hope. She's been sitting too long. We obviously have auxiliary power, but they're using an E6 field tap that's so primitive it makes my hair stand on end just being in the same ship with it. If we turned it on it might work...or it might not work—catastrophically." She shrugged. "Not really sure what you want to do."

Nate frowned thoughtfully. "What about the defensive systems? Are they patched into the computer?"

Shannon shook her head again. "Nope, and that's another reason I wouldn't want to move it. Who knows what would happen if the collision system really is tied to the moon? Wouldn't even care to guess."

Nate nodded. "I think we'll leave it here...*without* messing with the defenses."

Shannon agreed, and Nate went to search the next deck down with the others.

There were two other notable finds over the next hour. Most of the rooms they checked had obviously been used for colonists first, with the mounting points and plumbing for cold sleep chambers still sticking through floor and walls, capped off or coiled and secured with ancient, congealed rigger tape. There were also dust patterns on just about every surface that showed they had later been used for storage, probably of artifacts that Paul eventually removed, based on half-visible shapes in the dust.

As he emerged from the crawl way yet another deck below, a sharp exclamation drew Nate down a main passage. A moment later it was repeated, even more sharp and insistent. "No! Don't!" It was Shawna's voice, coming down yet another side passage. Again, Nate followed her cry into a completely unmarked side chamber that at first seemed exactly like all the others. The walls and ceiling were the same, but in the center of the room a column of something shiny jutted out of the floor. It wasn't metal, and might have been some kind of glass or crystal.

Atop it sat a gem that was roughly the size of Nate's head. It was so dark that it drank in all the light that surrounded it, looking more like a hole in reality than anything else Nate could imagine. Nate could see its facets only on one side, where the light reflected faintly from the sheer surface.

The more immediate concern was Keevan, who stood transfixed before it, his hand outstretched. Nate had arrived just in time or he might not have believed what he saw. Wisps of darkness reached out from that pitch-black void to meet Keevan's fingertips, as if to draw him in to touch it. He might have been sleepwalking, his motions slow and clumsy, as he shuffled forward the last step toward the strange object. Then he did touch it. When his skin contacted the gem, his body went completely rigid.

His head swiveled slowly, menacingly toward Shawna, who stood out of Nate's line of sight to one side of the room. The voice that issued from his lips was far too deep for his small frame. **"*So*... *Long*... *In The Darkkkkkk!*"**

Shawna was silent, as if whatever she saw in Keevan's eyes had rendered her speechless.

Nate's mind was racing, but he too was frozen in place, not sure how to respond.

Keevan spoke again, **"*I* *Am* *Jozriel.*"** Then, after a moment, **"*How Did You Come To My Prison, Human?*"** Shawna let out a strangled gasp, but still didn't speak. After a moment, Jozriel spoke again, its tone unmistakably impatient. **"*Humans... Were it possible I had forgotten how stupid and weak you are?**

Though the Maker's fiends locked us away so *Long* ago, still I should have remembered*."

Nate stepped forward into the doorway, so he could see Shawna clearly. She was gasping and clutching at her throat, and some movement of her hand must have brought the amulet hanging there to the creature's attention, because its next words seemed almost excited. **"*What..* *What is *this*??* *Who made you, little pretty?* *What luck!* *Hmmmm... Locked away, I see... But such power...* *Such.... *Power!**"**

The final, almost reverent note of Jozriel's monologue was cut short as Nate drifted forward through the doorway into the room and Keevan's head whipped around to stare at him.

It was, indeed, his eyes that were the most shocking. They were completely black, sucking in the light, just like the gem to which Keevan's hand was still affixed. His face was stuck in a rigid, grinning mask, almost like a caricature of a clown. Nate shivered involuntarily as those eyes widened even further, the horrifying light-devouring blackness eating yet more of Keevan's face. The harsh, sibilant voice, still far too deep and completely wrong for Keevan's vocal chords assaulted him directly. **"*Who are *you*?...* *What...*ARE* you?*"**

The huge, black eyes narrowed, which was somehow even worse than before, as if all the malevolent attention in the universe was focused out of their slitted aperture. **"*Yoou??? The *One*?? I should have guessed!!*"** It paused for a long moment. **"*But... How can this be? Do *They* know?? Did *They* foresee?!?!*"**

He stared for another long, frozen moment and let out a shriek so unearthly that Nate and Shawna both gave a violent start. "*The *Wyrm* tricked me!!! From the very beginning, it *knew*. Even before I was cursed to sightless imprisonment in this mortal hell!! For this, my children—my race—will *die*? This cannot stand! It *must not* stand!!*"

With that, Keevan moved so quickly Nate barely registered what he was doing. He certainly didn't have time to react before Keevan had lifted the enormous faceted gem and hurled it straight at Nate's head.

Nate's reflexive reaction, reaching out to slap the huge gem out of the air, was barely fast enough. There was a brilliant flash when his hand contacted it, leaving spots dancing in his vision, and somehow the flash reached beyond the spectrum of visible light. Nate's awareness of Energematrice6 was pierced with the same bright hole as his vision. The black gem, meanwhile, clanged off the metal bulkhead to his right and drifted off into the middle of the room.

Keevan dove for the object with a cry, but Shawna saw what he was doing and pushed off to intercept. She slammed into him, and the two hit the bulkhead in a tangle of arms and legs as Nate's vision began to clear.

Keevan squawked, "C'mon Shawna! We gotta take it with us! It's callin' to me, I'm tellin' ya!" He tried to disentangle himself, his eyes still fixed on the gem floating across the room behind Shawna.

"Keevan!" Nate barked, "What in the void is the matter with you?"

"Nate! Help!" Shawna's tone was fearful and she clung desperately to Keevan's arm.

Nate pushed off toward the gem where it floated across the room. As he traveled, he turned slowly toward Keevan, rotating his body. When he spun past, something in the surface of the gem caught his eye and seemed to stare back at him, leering. There was no time to wonder over it, though.

"Keevan! Snap out of it!" Nate's tone was full of command, but Keevan continued to babble.

"We've gotta to take it with us. Can't you see? It's..." Keevan cut off as Nate came between Keevan and the gem.

"I think not." Nate said. "In fact, Keevan, go see what else you can find. Now."

Keevan frowned and started to open his mouth again, but then he really saw the look on Nate's face, and finally it penetrated his near-mania. He blinked in surprise, then frowned uncertainly and shook his head, as if to clear it. "I guess... Yeah, sure." He turned reluctantly away and pushed off toward the hatch where they'd come in, rubbing his palm.

Shawna had turned to stare at the gem as Nate touched down on the "wall" and rebounded back toward the door, his own wary gaze now fixed on the gem, floating in the back corner of the room, and she asked in a quiet voice, "What? What...is it?"

Nate shook his head grimly, his own expression bleak. "I'm not precisely sure, but I don't think it's something I want any of us touching ever again."

Keevan didn't wait for them outside the hatch, instead swinging into another room down the corridor.

Once he and Shawna were both outside, Nate closed the hatch himself and locked it, keying a code into the electronic lock. Shawna looked at Nate, frowning. "Was that... One of *Them*? Caught in that gem?"

Nate stared back at her for a long moment, frowning. "Or maybe something worse. I wish I knew...or maybe I don't." He shook his head. "No safer place for it than here, and I'm not taking it with us."

One final find, from Laura, distracted them. She came from another room, yet another level down, holding what at first looked like a fist-size cylinder. When she handed it to Nate, however, it became obvious that it was a set of disks, bound together by an unseen force that, when Nate examined the object with Energematrice6, might or might not have been directly related to the energy fields. There was Energematrice6 flowing through it, but the configuration was strange and it didn't respond to Nate's prodding. Nate shrugged and agreed that it too should be taken along.

The room in which Laura had found the disks was another puzzle. It was still in use as a storage room, but none of the other objects inside were directly linked to Energematrice6 in any unusual fashion. They were just ordinary gems or simple machines, like a microscope and a bank of computers that might or might not still function.

When they had examined the rest of the ship and found nothing of note, they were all getting tired, but Jon and Rachel were still in their father's old cabin.

When Nate went to check on them, he found them just sitting, staring at a metal ring that hung in the air between them. It was a plain band with no inscription or markings, but there were tears in Rachel's eyes and hovering in tiny droplets around her face and Jon looked heartsick.

Rachel saw Nate and she let out a choked sob. "It's his wedding ring. He left it for us. He's gone." She broke down again, crying quietly.

Jon grimaced, then said without looking at Nate, "He loved mom so much. He never let her go. Even though she died when we were too young to remember, he talked about her all the time like she was still there."

Nate closed the hatch behind him and floated there, looking at the ring thoughtfully. After a long moment, Jon continued, "The fact that he left that for us means he really thought he was going to die. There's no other way he would have done it." He turned his head toward Nate, his face drained of color.

Rachel dashed the tears from her eyes, using one hand to steady herself, and shook her head. "He can't be. He just can't. We'll find him."

Nate pushed off gently from where he clung to the hatch and caught himself next to Rachel, then enfolded her in a hug made awkward by the lack of gravity. "Is that what he'd want you to do?"

Rachel sighed. "No. Of course not. He told us *not* to, but we can't give up on him."

Nate bit his lip, but he shook his head. "Rach, you're not giving up on him. If I know you at all, you never will, but you only have so much time in this world. What was your dad doing with his time?"

Rachel shook her head in denial for a moment, but then she looked Nate right in the eyes and he could feel her heart breaking as she answered, "He was fighting against the evil Lastis released into the world. His whole life, that's all he did—fight to save people from it and fight it himself, but there was never anybody to look after *him*."

Nate nodded, frowning. "So what did he want you to do?"

Rachel shook her head again, obviously resisting what she said, even as she said it, "He always said 'There are only two paths in life. We can fight against evil or to fight for it, by action or inaction.'" She stopped for a moment, then looked at Nate through tear-fogged eyes. "He said those were the only two choices we have."

Nate nodded again, grimly. "He was right...and so are you. Someone should take care of him." Nate paused for a long moment, giving Rachel another squeeze then reaching over to lay a hand on Jon's arm. "Be sure what you choose to do doesn't waste the time you have."

Rachel finally hugged Nate back, fiercely. Nate returned her embrace, then released her, allowing himself to drift toward the ceiling as she turned to regard her father's ring again, her face finally relaxing. Nate pushed off of the ceiling to flip himself around and move toward the door.

Behind him, Rachel said quietly, "He wanted us to help you, when you arrived, and we will."

He turned his head as he reached the door and nodded to her with a grave, quiet smile. "We have so much to do, you can't even imagine."

The trip back to Adamant was mostly uneventful, though they could find no simple way to move the artifact that controlled the Vale, christened unimaginatively by Tye the 'Globe of the Vale.' After some discussion, Tye volunteered to hold it while they towed him across the gap with a length of line. That accomplished, they went through the process of cycling through Adamant's airlock yet again.

Once back aboard, Nate went to secure the Globe of the Vale in his own cabin.

At first, he couldn't find an appropriate place to put it. It was just large enough that none of the storage compartments, even the closet, would fit it. Eventually, he decided that securing it to the sleeping couch with the restraint netting was his best option.

That done, he made his way to the bridge where Andrew was examining the others' amulets with fascination. With a smile, Nate offered him a choice of the remaining four. At first, Andrew looked nervous, and even quickly passing his hand over each to feel the Energematrice6 flowing through them left him sweating, but he seemed genuinely grateful when he chose the yellow amulet. When he put it on, it lit up with a soft golden light.

"Andrew," Nate asked, "what's bothering you?"

Andrew's lips twisted. "I used to be good at this."

Nate simply waited while Andrew sat staring at his new amulet.

After a long moment, Andrew said, "I almost killed myself. We always just called it overexertion. It's what you call entropic shock. It was when we were running away. Back...home? Makes me wish I had one of those." He eyed Nate's Rechemacula dolefully.

Nate nodded, and Andrew shook his head. "It was... bad. There was no time to rest when I did it, and ever since..." He shook his head again. "Ever since, I can hardly stand to open my senses to it. I know it's all in my head, but I just can't."

Shawna spoke up from where she was strapped in, "Andy, you saved us so many times. Whatever you can't do, it's not because you're weak."

Andrew barked a laugh. "Oh I don't have any regrets. I did what I had to do, but now?"

He shrugged helplessly, then looked up into Nate's face. "I can barely stand to even look at it now."

Nate nodded. "We'll find a way to help you. There's not time right now, but we will find it."

Jon looked at Andrew sadly. "I can't heal entropic shock, you know. I've tried."

Tye snorted. "You and everybody else." He smiled sympathetically at Andrew. "Just be glad you didn't hurt yourself physically. The physical part is even harder to heal than the mental part. The professors could help people whose minds were...stuck, like yours."

As they all secured themselves for travel, Rachel stared through the great window at Hope One from two seats to Nate's left. "I almost wish I could stay."

Next to her, Jon shook his head. "And do what, Rach?"

She shook her own head mutely in turn as Laura laid a hand on her arm from the other side. Laura's eyes were more than a bit haunted as she turned to Rachel. "I know how you feel." She squeezed Rachel's hand.

Jon, too, squeezed her hand and Rachel turned her head to give him a crooked grin. "At least we're not trapped in a crystal anymore."

"Speaking of which," Nate was frowning. "We had a little incident aboard Hope." He relayed to them all what had happened with Keevan and Shawna and the black gem. When he'd finished, Keevan was staring at him as if he'd never seen him before.

"I don't remember any of that." Keevan shook his head emphatically, absentmindedly rubbing his hand. "I swear. I would never." He looked troubled, and shook his head again, almost reflexively.

Nate nodded grimly, "It was messing with your mind. If you'd seen what we saw... Well." He shrugged.

Shawna looked scared, presumably at even the memory of what had happened.

"I'd never." Keevan seemed almost desperate now, and Jesse reached over to lay a hand on his shoulder. "It's all right, Raddink. You have friends around you."

Keevan looked at Jesse for a moment, nonplussed, then laughed aloud. "Imagine! A Galton saying that to me! Am I dreamin'?" Jesse smiled, but his own gaze had turned inward, presumably to his own memories. Finally he blurted, "Nate, I messed up."

Nate frowned and nodded for him to continue. Keevan squirmed, then said, "I told 'em too much. They pushed me, and I'm not good at sayin' no. I tried. I mean, I grew up with these people, some of em. I'm sorry..." He looked desperate, as if he were trying to escape something.

Jesse snorted, "What? ...Who did you tell? and what did you say?"

Keevan squirmed again and hung his head, "It was Rebus. I told 'im you'd killed a Changed. I told 'im you'd banished the Shade. When you escaped from Loriden."

"Rebus." Jesse scowled and his gaze darkened. "When they told me you wanted me to come with I wondered if he was behind it somehow. What could he be playing at?"

Nate looked at Jesse quizzically. "I asked? ...That was Rebus' idea." His lips twisted ironically. "Not that I mind having you along. You were more than welcome."

Jesse had gone pale, though, and he shook his head.

"We have to get back. Rebus is up to something, and we have to stop him."

Nate sighed and shook his head, then turned to Keevan. "I didn't escape from Loriden. I left. ...and I forgive you, Keevan." He looked over to Jesse. "We'll head back, but don't be surprised if our welcome isn't worn out."

Jesse shook his head stubbornly, "My father would never allow something like this. Rebus is going too far."

When they had all settled in, Andrew took the helm to head them all back toward Lighthouse Station. The trip back through Hope One's collision field was slow and might have been painful if they weren't all exhausted from their search. As it was, every one of them was in a near-stupor as Andrew inched them back out of Hope One's field then turned her attention to navigating around the primary toward Lighthouse Station.

As they traveled, Nate studied the clouds of the Vale around them. Was there less movement? Less density? He wasn't certain, but it seemed to him that there must be. Or he was imagining it. How could he compare when he hadn't known to look in the first place?

After they left the collision field, it took an hour to get back to Lighthouse Station. When they arrived, they docked at their previous berth and again waited for the docking mechanisms to complete their seal. As they moved to debark, Nate traded a glance with Jesse, then said, "You should all stay here... except Jesse. We'll go see whether we're welcome anymore."

Andrew looked at him askance. "Is that wise?"

Nate read agreement with Andrew in the eyes of several of the others, but he just shook his head. "What do you think they're going to do?" Andrew didn't look convinced, but the rest of the little group didn't follow when Nate turned and pushed himself toward the airlock. As he pushed the button to open it, he turned back to them, his mouth quirked wryly. "One way or another, I doubt this will take long."

When Nate emerged from the airlock into the station, there was, again, a greeting party. This time, however, it was two of the council members with no crowd or fanfare. Elders Rebus and Eden stood stiffly, their backs straight, and Nate couldn't help feeling that they were looking down their noses at him from the very moment he left the airlock. Nate also couldn't help noticing the two security guards that loomed behind them, their faces blank.

"Nate," Rebus said, stepping forward. "The council would ask that you and any of your companions who wish to come back aboard Lighthouse station accompany us to a full session of the council."

Nate's eyebrows rose and he frowned, but then he nodded thoughtfully, "I can do that."

Immediately upon following Nate out of the airlock, Jesse saw Rebus and Eden and scowled. "Are you two making trouble again?" He looked over at Nate. "I wondered if I should have stayed here just to see that they couldn't do anything...stupid."

Rebus smirked. "The council is convened and waiting. Best come along, Jesse."

Nate spent the ten minute walk in melancholy contemplation. He had enjoyed his comparatively short stay on Lighthouse station, and he got the distinct feeling that time would soon be coming to an end, whether he liked it or not. By contrast, Jesse was visibly fuming beside him.

As they approached the conclave, its main door now guarded by two strong-looking men, Nate laid a hand on Jesse's arm. "Let me do the talking." Jesse nodded reluctantly as they were ushered through.

"...urge you toward reason." Elder Strong was speaking as they stepped into the conclave, but she broke off at the sight of them. The podium at the bottom center of the room had been removed, replaced by chairs for each member of the council...except Jesse.

Rebus and Eden led them down the main aisle toward the council, which sat in a semicircle facing them, with two empty spaces. Looking awkward, Rebus and Eden hurried down the aisle to take their places in those empty chairs, leaving Nate and Jesse to walk the last few yards by themselves. Nate glanced over at Jesse and smiled crookedly, continuing to move at a dignified pace. The auditorium around them was once again filled with the people of Lighthouse Station, though from Jesse's dark glances around, Nate wondered if the crowd had been gathered a bit selectively.

When he reached the dais, Nate stepped up onto the circular platform in the center of the room directly across from the council and promptly sat down cross legged facing them. Most looked a bit shocked as he did, evidently having expected him to remain standing like a criminal come for justice. Elder Jaben frowned thoughtfully and Elder Strong's eyes widened and crinkled at the corners. She managed to suppress her smile, but it was a near thing.

Jesse stood for a moment, looking around at the council with a mixture of confusion and hurt, hardening after a moment into a deep anger. As Jesse took a position beside Nate, also cross legged, Jaben spoke, "Nate, we find that there is some...question regarding your status and we wish to make a formal inquiry."

Rebus broke in, "How rapidly do you age, boy?"

Jaben gave Rebus an annoyed look and continued as smoothly as he could, "There are allegations that you are..." He paused uncomfortably, "an 'Odd.'"

Jaben's discomfort intensified, but he soldiered on, "There has also been suggestion that you are not, as claimed, the Brightstar." He trailed off, frowning at Nate.

Nate nodded slowly, then shrugged. He looked Jaben in the eye. "I am who I am. You can call me whatever name you choose. It was the Keeper, your own leader, who gave me this." He held up the Sigil of Mysteries, which glowed softly even in the bright light of the auditorium. "Tell me, from where do you take the name 'Brightstar?'"

Surprisingly, it was Eden who spoke in response, "From the prophecies of the Wildman, Siever Radding." His eyes were fixed on Nate as he continued, "Many know of the prophecies of Radding, given at the Telestry. It is his most famous prophecy, 'Darkness before you and chaos behind you, in hubris and weakness the bright star will blind you,' from which we take the name Brightstar."

Eden looked at Nate hard as he continued, "What few know is that we, too, were given a sign, when Radding pierced the Vale upon his third Rejection. The words have been preserved, passed down through the council and through my own family. They are not known widely—have never been uttered before a full session of the council, even, but they have been kept as a surety against the day of Brightstar's appearance."

Eden paused for a moment, likely reciting in his own head. When he spoke again, he was obviously quoting long-rehearsed and oft-repeated memory, "Like a filing to the lodestone, the light of goodness draws him. His only home within the Vale, an elder spring of truth and lore. To the people he gives praise and to council respect and honor their due."

As Eden finished, Rebus rose to his feet. He had obviously been waiting for the cue, because he pointed accusingly at Nate. "Disrespect. Disrespect is all you have shown the council! 'Elder spring of truth'? Fah. The drivel you spread among the people is as foul as you are, Odd! Brightstar you most certainly are not!"

Beside Nate, Jesse jumped to his feet. "You would defy my father openly!?! When he returns..."

Nate interrupted Jesse without seeming to raise his voice, but still driving past his outburst, "Peace, Jesse."

Nate shook his head slowly, then looked each member of the council in the eye in turn before he spoke, "'No prophet is accepted in his own country.' The Wild Man was rejected by the Telestry, not once but three times for giving them more truth than he gave to anyone else in the galaxy. Likewise, I gave you the truth more plainly than I may anywhere else, and you reject it." There were mutters from the audience behind Nate, and the council's faces grew, if possible, even more stony than they had been before.

Jaben shook his head in rejection. "You defied the council directly, Nate Brightstar, and your... history lesson... left more unrest among the people of Sanctuary than we have had in my entire lifetime."

Nate rose to his feet. Though he was still shorter than any of them, seated as they were in their tall council chairs, Nate might have towered over them. "Long after this universe is lost to memory, an unwelcome truth will still be the most potent insult it is possible for one person to offer another. Ancient lore from Earth itself tells you that wisdom loves correction, but a fool wants nothing more than to hear his own words in another's mouth."

Rebus looked on the brink of speaking again, his face growing red, but Nate continued, "The truth is that the people of Sanctuary lead the most privileged life in the galaxy. Because you are protected by the Vale, unopposed and unassailable, this council has become arrogant, even if your people are not.

"I paid you every respect you deserved. You cannot say the same about your treatment of me. Just as your prophecy says, I gave this council a come-down, exactly as you were due. It was the greatest gift I could offer you."

Apparently, Rebus could take no more. He broke in with a yell, "Take him!" With his utterance, Rebus's eyes changed, his pupils stretching into vertical slits. He stepped forward and stared into Nate's eyes, his voice dropping to a near whisper, "I KNOW what you ARE…'Brightstar'."

Behind Nate, several people from the crowd rose up and stormed up the stairs while Nate stood frozen, his gaze locked with Rebus's, his attention shattering. Rebus knew. Nate could see it in those exsect eyes. He knew about both of Nate's worlds. He knew what Nate really was.

Then the crowd was there, seizing Nate by the arms and around the middle, hefting him easily above their heads. For a moment, Nate was afraid they were going to actually tear him apart. He instinctively tried to seize

Energematrice6 to defend himself. His mind was stuck in the same paralysis that was so familiar to his body in that other reality. He could see Energematrice6 as clearly as ever, but grasping it was so far beyond him in his shattered state, he didn't even know where to begin. He could no more use the fields than he could have done a handspring or even tied his own shoes in that other, impossibly distant world. Terror and confusion enveloped him as his helplessness in the grasp of those below struck home and he thrashed uselessly.

"To the locks!" one of them yelled. There was a general roar of approval and the whole mass started moving, carrying him along. From where he was held above the crowd, as if from a world away, Nate could see Jesse's mouth drop open in shock. He also caught a glimpse of Rebus's gloating sneer. As the crowd turned, now joined by others from the surrounding amphitheater, Nate heard Jaben fruitlessly trying to impose his voice over their roar.

Nate's own shock at Rebus's revelation and a gut-wrenching feeling of failure prolonged his paralysis as the same four men held him over their heads, carrying him bodily through the station while the rest of the mob forced gawkers out of their way.

More than once as the eternity of the next minute or two wore on and a sense of unreality overcame his paralysis, Nate tried again to use Energematrice6, hoping to simply incapacitate the mob that carried him down the corridor. They were none too gentle, and the only thing he was certain of was that they were up to no good. If they were on their way to the airlock, as their words had suggested, that most likely meant another trip through the vacuum without gear. Over the time it took for the mob to reach the nearest airlock, on the opposite side of the station's hub from where Adamant was berthed, Nate struggled savagely against the wall that kept him from grasping the fields. Even as his shock wore off, something else stopped him. At first he thought it was the same paralysis that had gripped him when Rebus had caught his eyes, and the same sense of horror and failure reached up to strangle him. Slowly, he realized it wasn't. He could see Energematrice6. He had opened his senses to it, but something was stopping him from using it against these people. The realization of what that wall was came to him in a flash as they rounded the last corner and he saw the airlock ahead of them. It was the Great Schemic itself. With that realization, Nate's focus came clear and his grasp of Energematrice6 was instantaneous. His original instinct, to stop the mob that held him, was still impossible for him for reasons he couldn't quite understand, but he prepared himself for what he knew must be coming. When they reached the airlock, one of their number had run ahead to cycle it open, and they shoved him unceremoniously inside.

Well, Nate thought, a little space walk wasn't going to hurt him, whatever they thought.

As the door was closing, he shaped the fields and, with his hand on the outside door, created a bubble around himself as quickly as he could, starting at his head and rapidly inflating to hold the rest of his body. This time, he didn't have to create his own air, only envelope the air already around him to hold it as the airlock depressurized.

He had barely finished when, a few seconds later, the door between him and the vacuum simply opened. Someone must have hit an emergency button, because the airlock hadn't cycled. The air was still inside the chamber, until suddenly it wasn't. The explosive decompression ripped Nate out of the airlock and tossed him into space...